Not Guilty

NOT QUITE A LADY

Helena Korin

Not Quite a Lady Copyright © 2018 by Helena Korin. All Rights Reserved.

Contents

Not Quite a Lady
vii

Acknowledgements
viii

Also by Helena Korin:
ix

Dedication
x

Disclaimer
xi

Chapter One
1

Chapter Two
16

Chapter Three
31

Chapter Four
41

Chapter Five
53

Chapter Six
64

Chapter Seven
78

Chapter Eight
89

Chapter Nine
97

Chapter Ten
107

Chapter Eleven
116

A word about the author
124
Afterword
125

Not Quite a Lady
Book #2 of English Garden Series

HELENA KORIN

Ruby Gillingham, a country girl from Kent, is traveling to London for the Little Season. Her father is Sir Roderick of Thorncroft Hall but her mother is not to be mentioned. Ruby has agreed to go because she hopes to catch the eye of Crispin, Lord Sayward, a most handsome English gentleman. He should be in London then, but will his mother, the dragon, discover that Ruby is 'not quite a lady'? There is also Peter, Lord Berringon, with the Irish lilt to his speech. He made her heart beat a little faster but he is back in Kent and with every hoof beat London is coming closer.

Acknowledgements

I wish to thank Stephanie Webb, my story editor, for her skilful guidance and my beta reader, Joanna Qureshi for catching my slip-ups. Also a thank you to Mimi Barbour for her helpfulness. Ladies what would I do without you?

Also by Helena Korin:

- Grandon Hall: A mystery set in an English country house party.
- An Orchid for Penelope: Can an Amazon adventurer find happiness with an English rose?

Dedication

For Lena and ReJean my cherished cheerleaders, who always have time to listen.

Disclaimer

This is a work of fiction. Names, characters, places, and incidents are either the product of the author's imagination or are used fictitiously, and any resemblance to actual persons living or dead, business establishments, events, or locales, is entirely coincidental.

Not Quite a Lady by Helena Korin

No part of this book may be used or reproduced in any manner whatsoever without the written permission of the author except in the case of brief quotations embodied in critical articles or reviews.

Chapter One

Kent 1819

Wincing with pain Ruby hobbled to the pond in the woods and sat down on a rock. She reached down, released her garter and pulled off her stocking. As she slipped her foot into the cool water she let out a sigh of relief. That felt so much better. She had obviously sprained her ankle when she fell a few minutes ago. The ground was slick from last night's rain and she had been too busy gathering the fragrant linden blossoms to watch where she was going. Heaving another sigh, contentment this time, she looked around. This was one of her favourite spots in the woods, it was like her own private world where she could sit in the shade on a quiet afternoon daydreaming as she trailed her hands in the water. Then she heard a sound. Who could it be? A man's voice, rich and mellow floated over the clear air as he sang about a faithless dairymaid. But who was he? And what was he doing at her pool? She peeked around the wild raspberry bushes and saw a man's curly dark head. She tried to hide, to slide further into the bushes so that he wouldn't see her but instead she felt herself slipping down the rock into the pond. She tried to catch herself, flailing around with her arms to grasp something to hold onto. "Oh! Help!" she cried.

Suddenly a strong arm grasped her around the waist and pulled her to safety, back up onto a flat rock. She found herself staring into the vivid blue eyes of a gentleman wearing a white shirt and neck cloth. "Who are you?" Ruby gasped.

"Peter, Lord Berrington, at your service," he said. "But are you all right? I heard you cry out."

"It's my ankle. I think I may have sprained it and wanted to soak it in cold water." She realized he was staring at her bare foot. "You aren't supposed to look!" she snapped as she pulled down her lace trimmed petticoat and mud spattered skirt.

"I'm sorry but how could I resist? You have beautiful feet." Then he laughed out loud. "Assuming, of course, that your other foot is as lovely as this one."

"Thank you, I think," she replied. Realizing that it seemed silly to stay angry with him she carried on. "I am glad you happened to come by the pond. I don't know how long I would have been stranded here."

"Ah, 'tis always my pleasure to help a damsel in distress. I was on my morning walk and I decided to explore the extent of my new domain, Linden Hall," he said, a smile hovering around his lips.

"I'm Ruby Gillingham of Thorncroft Hall. My father is Sir Roderick. Wait... did you just say you live at Linden Hall? But it's been vacant for years. Did you arrive recently?" she asked. What a handsome man. He was clean-shaven and very pleasing to look at.

"Yes, just last month. The lawyers finally discovered that I'm the next of kin and tracked me down. Ireland's been my home until now."

"That explains why you speak the way you do. I'm sorry – that wasn't meant as a criticism," she added. "But you have an almost musical rhythm of speech."

"Aye. 'Tis my Irish childhood." He gave Ruby another smile and something melted inside her. She liked this man. Does Linden Hall need many repairs?" she asked.

"Yes, actually, it does. But one wing is habitable so I'm staying there with a skeleton staff while the plasterers fix the walls and the chimneys are swept, that sort of thing."

"What are the gardens like?"

"Very overgrown, I'm afraid, but there are some roses and fruit trees amidst the briers. It must have been a lovely estate once."

Ruby nodded. "I'd like to see it one day. Anyone who planted that avenue of lime trees must have been a gardener at heart. Have you considered building an orangery or a glasshouse? Brambley Hall, nearby, has a beautiful one and the owner, Mr. Greenley, grows the most exquisite orchids."

"I've heard about glasshouses but first I must see about basics like growing oats and barley. How is your foot now? Should we try getting you into your carriage?"

"Yes. It feels much better, thank you." Ruby slipped on her stocking but gave up when it came to her half boot. She'd carry it.

Peter slipped one arm around her waist and his other arm under her knees. She felt herself lifted as if she weighed little more than a porcelain doll. He carried her up the path and placed her in the passenger seat of her tilbury. He untied Poppy, her mare, and climbed into the carriage beside her.

"I dare say you could drive yourself home without mishap, but I'd feel better knowing that you got there safely," he said.

"Thank you. I appreciate that." She was very aware of his body snugged up next to hers. As they took a curve in the road she couldn't help sliding closer still, enjoying the secure feeling it gave her. He smelled of the outdoors mixed with soap and leather. Then the heady perfume of the Linden trees overwhelmed her again. "Oh, how I love this avenue of trees," Ruby said "I would bottle their perfume if I could and look, do you see all the tiny heart-shaped leaves between the clusters of white flowers?"

"Aye, 'tis pleasant, I agree, but what will your father think when he finds a stranger bringing you home?"

Ruby turned and smiled, "He will ask you many questions but when he finds you're a neighbour he'll likely offer you a drink."

"A man after my own heart."

"I'll be leaving for London in a few days and I'll miss all this." She waved her hand to indicate the meadow washed with the new green of spring and bright yellow daffodils nodding in the breeze.

"You're not happy to go?"

"No, I'm not. But my father and my aunt insist."

"What about your mother?"

"She died seven years ago."

"I'm that sorry, lass."

Ruby and Peter drove down the rutted country road then turned onto a smoother, well-travelled one.

"Do you have family in Ireland?" she asked.

"Just my brother. But my sister is in London now,

staying with her godparents. What about you? Are you part of a large happy family?"

"No. I have one half-brother at Cambridge but he's a lot older."

"It sounds lonely."

"It was a little, but my father and I spend a lot of time together and I enjoy walking in all kinds of weather and look," she pointed across the field. "There are new lambs."

"Aye. I too love the countryside but I have concerns about the peasantry."

"Peasantry? Oh, you must mean tenant farmers," she said. "But why the concern? My father treats his people well."

"That's not what happens where I come from," he replied with a somber look. "Now, where do I turn off?"

"Just past that oak tree." She pointed to the left as the manor house of Thorncroft Hall came into view, it's weathered bricks so old and familiar to her. They drove into the yard and before Ruby even considered how best to get out and into the house without hurting her ankle further, Peter picked her up and strode to the entrance. Stanson, the butler, answered, a look of astonishment on his face. "Miss Ruby?" he managed to stammer.

Just then her father appeared in the doorway. "What's this? Who is this man and why is he carrying you?"

"Father, I slipped and hurt my ankle down by the stream. This is Lord Berrington who has kindly helped me get home." She twisted her neck to look up at her rescuer and completed the introductions, "This is my father, Lord Roderick."

"I'm happy to meet you, sir," Berrington said trying to nod in lieu of bowing.

"Humph. Well, put her down in here." Her father led

the way to the drawing room and indicated the settee. Berrington did as asked and immediately slid a footstool in front of her.

"Thank you, milord," Ruby said.

"You don't live around here, do you, young man?" her father asked.

"I have just inherited Linden Hall but I grew up near Dublin in Ireland."

"I see. Then you are new to our neighborhood. I'm sure we will run into each other again. Thank you for coming to my daughter's aid. Good day to you, sir." Her father did not smile.

"It was my pleasure. Good day, sir." Berrington bowed and left at once. Mounting his horse in one fluid motion he trotted down the road, then spurred his horse to a gallop. Ruby watched him from the window until he disappeared over the hill and out of sight. What an interesting new neighbour. It really was too bad that she couldn't get to know him a little better before she left for London.

"Didn't you like him, father?" she asked, surprised at his behaviour because he was usually congenial and more hospitable.

"No, Ruby. I have my reasons, which have nothing to do with you. All you need to know is that I don't care for the Irish," he replied as he walked briskly out of the parlour, leaving Ruby in confusion.

***

Berrington rode down the avenue of linden trees to his new home, Miss Ruby Gillingham very much on his mind. She was no shrinking violet, driving herself around the countryside and dipping her bare feet into the pond with a stranger watching. He could still remember how she felt in his arms. Yes. He wanted to see her again. But she was leaving for London in a few days. Perhaps he should go to London, too? His sister would be happy to see him. Berrington appreciated his good fortune. If all the male relatives on his mother's side of the family hadn't died out, he would still be working for his cousin, Roger, in Glendalough, Ireland. Ever since he'd begun studying law at Oxford they had argued long and hard about Roger's treatment of his tenants. Roger insisted that the peasants were used to their lot in life and his estate would lose money if he changed their living conditions. Berrington didn't agree and fortunately, now he would have the chance to apply some of his more liberal ideas. From the little that Miss Gillingham had said, things were not the same here as in Ireland; farmers were not exploited.

He looked forward to the challenges that lay ahead. He could see that Linden Hall had a lot of potential but it had been left to stagnate far too long. Much needed to be done, in the house and garden, but at the moment his main concern were the crops. He didn't know the climate in this part of Kent. What should be planted this late in the season? He'd need a manager but where to find someone who agreed with his ideas on estate management? Perhaps Lord Dabbley, his sister's godfather in London, could advise? Once he had sorted things out at Linden Hall and made some improvements, he'd have time to court some pretty ladies, the delightful Miss Ruby Gillingham in particular. Smiling to himself, Berrington dismounted at his stable and went to check on the progress of the workmen in his house.

The entrance to Linden Hall had been freshly painted in a pale cream colour and the oak panelling gently gleamed after a polishing. The flooring needed some new tiles in places but apparently the fireplace now drew well.

Good. He went up the stairwell and turned to the right. He had chosen the largest bedroom for himself and now he opened its casement window. Over the garden wall he could see glimpses of the River Wistwell meandering its way through a flower-filled meadow. The workmen had been mending fences, and his stallion, Arthur, grazed in the far pasture. He looked down, on the enclosed garden where a fountain stood in crumbling, overgrown shambles — more needed repair. The fountain would be the focal point of this area and something he would see each morning.

His list of improvements kept growing so, before leaving for London, he would need to talk to his foreman about the next project. Much of the furniture needed to be replaced, too. Mice had made nests in the mattresses and the one settee was no longer usable. The table in the dining room was still solid however. He made a mental list of what he would need to purchase. Going downstairs he found the cook in the kitchen. The woman stood with her back to him and whirled around when he spoke. "Mrs. Banbury, what do you need most urgently in the kitchen and for the dining room?"

"Oh, milord! I didn't know you were back. You startled me," she said bobbing a curtsey.

"But yes, milord, you need dishes, tankards and wine goblets. If you were to have even four guests, right now, there aren't enough dishes to feed them and your guests would have to share the wine bottle." She smiled at him.

"Would you know about the bedding?"

"I think you need to replace that too, milord. Most of it, I fear."

"I will attend to it, then. Thank you, Mrs. Banbury. I shall leave for London tomorrow."

***

The next day Ruby climbed into a lovely carriage, which smelled of leather and freshly curried horses. Jonathan Greenley, her friend Penelope's husband, had offered to convey Ruby to London since he needed to make the trip himself. Mr. Greenley was a pleasant man but spent most of their journey perusing a botany text, which gave her ample opportunity to consider her own secret reason for agreeing to this London Season. It was Crispin, Lord Sayward. She had met him months ago before he sailed off to Haiti on a plant collecting expedition. Tall, well built, she still remembered how her pulse raced when his beautiful grey eyes had met her own. Perhaps if she learned to be more of a lady he would find her attractive? Then there was the newly arrived Lord Berrington. Her father didn't seem to like him but she would have welcomed a chance to get to know him better, too. There was something warm and friendly about him but he was back in Kent and with every hoof beat London was coming closer.

When their carriage stopped at a posting inn and they had alighted, Mr. Greenley at last struck up a conversation. "I understand that this is your first trip to London," he said.

"Yes. I'm not sure what to expect. Is it as big as they say?"

"Bigger, with smoke-filled air, foul smells and crowded noisy streets. That's how I'd describe London," he said.

"You make it sound terrible," Ruby said smiling at his blunt honesty.

"It's no secret that I prefer the country though occasionally I must go into the city. But your experience may be different, for you will be going to dances and other social gatherings. Young ladies seem to enjoy that sort of thing. I'm fortunate that Penelope didn't long for a Season."

"But I thought the whole point of a Season was to find a husband and she had already met you."

"Yes, I repeat. I was fortunate. Do you know this aunt you'll be staying with?"

"No, not really. I think we met when I was a child." Ruby started biting her bottom lip. What would her aunt be like? And how would she treat her niece, the niece with the inconvenient mother? Suddenly she had less appetite. She looked down at her plate. The meat pie was tasty and who knew how long it would be before they reached London? Pragmatically, she washed it down with a strong cup of tea and went outside to stretch her legs.

Soon it was time to mount into the carriage again. As the afternoon wore on she dozed off, lulled by the rhythmic sway of the coach. She awoke to someone shouting outside the carriage over a din of other noises that assaulted her from all sides. The yelling came from a young boy hawking his newspapers. She stretched and peered out of the window. She had never seen such a crowd of people before nor heard such a racket on the street.

"Welcome to London, Miss Gillingham," Mr. Greenley said with a wry smile.

"You told me that the streets were noisy but I didn't expect this."

"We're on the outskirts of the city. Soon we will be in quieter residential areas. Ah, here we are on Sloane Street. It's an area for the nouveau riche. Your aunt lives in Mayfair which is in an older very respectable part of town." The carriage stopped at 647 Crescent Street and Mr. Greenley escorted Ruby to her aunt's front door.

"Mr. Greenley and Miss Gillingham to see Lady Paxton," he said handing his card to the butler when he answered the door.

"Her ladyship is expecting you, sir. Please, come this way." The butler said leading them into the drawing room to announce them.

An older woman stood up as they entered. She had a pleasant expression and bore a strong resemblance to Ruby's father. Her grey-streaked hair was pulled up into a tight bun on the top of her head and a few curls framed her face. She curtseyed as Mr. Greenley gave a correct bow. Ruby quickly followed suit and bobbed a curtsey too. She noticed that her aunt moved stiffly as if she had a backache or perhaps her corset was laced too tightly?

"Welcome Mr. Greenley, it is kind of you to bring my niece to me. Ruby, child, I haven't seen you since you were a babe in arms. My, you've grown to be quite tall." She gave her a quick smile then turned back to Mr. Greenley. "Will you stay to tea, Sir? I understand you are a botanist and have expert advice for those who are interested in those new glasshouses."

"Thank you, my lady, but I can't stop. I'm expected at Lord Tollhouse's London residence this evening. He is building a conservatory in Sussex and wishes a consultation." He turned to Ruby. "I leave you in good hands, Miss Gillingham. Until we meet again." He bowed to them both and departed.

Her aunt turned to her with a welcoming smile. "Come, sit by the fire. Tell me. Are you as excited as I am about your first Season?"

"Yes, ma'am, I think so, but I've led a very quiet life in

the country up till now," Ruby said trying to look happy although the prospect of meeting many strangers terrified her. Knowing her social standing might be considered less than acceptable didn't help.

"Well now, you must be ready for a change. I understand you were at boarding school for a few years. Which one?"

"St. Ursula's, ma'am."

"Ah yes, it has a good reputation so they should have covered the basics. While we're waiting for the tea to arrive, please walk over to the window and back for me. I want to assess your posture." Ruby did as she was told, feeling rather self-conscious.

"Very good. You can sit down. You move well but need to slow your gait a little. Ladies should never hurry unless it's absolutely necessary. Tomorrow we must visit my modiste. You need a new wardrobe as soon as possible." At Ruby's surprised look she added. "What is suitable for country wear is not suitable for the city."

When tea arrived, with paper-thin cucumber sandwiches and a delicious looking pound cake, Ruby loaded her plate and happily took the first bite. Then she noticed her aunt looking askance and saw that Aunt Ada had only one small sandwich on her plate. After sipping at her tea and nibbling on her sandwich, Aunt Ada pushed her plate away and looked expectantly at Ruby. Puzzled, Ruby quickly placed her plate on the table beside her, gazing longingly at the enticing slice of the pound cake that remained on it.

"What are your accomplishments, child?"

"Accomplishments, ma'am?" Ruby asked in confusion.

"What do you do to entertain yourself? Do you sing or paint, embroider, dance, play the pianoforte or the harp, perhaps?"

"I'm told that I sing nicely and I like to draw, ma'am." Then she added, "Oh yes, and I've done some country dancing."

"First of all, Ruby, call me Aunt Ada or just aunt, not ma'am. If you don't know how to dance anything other than a reel, dancing lessons will be first on the agenda. And please do try to control your appetite. A young girl like you should have a smaller waistline. Your clothes will fit so much better, too."

"I'll try ma'am, I mean Aunt Ada," Ruby said giving the pound cake on her plate another wistful glance.

"Abby will see you to your room and help you unpack. Dinner is at eight o'clock. Meet me in the drawing room at ten minutes to eight, precisely."

Ruby followed the maid up the stairs. Eight o' clock seemed late for dinner, she was used to country hours with dinner at six. However would she last until then with only two tiny sandwiches and a bite of pound cake to sustain her? The maid opened her suitcase and started to unpack her clothes but Ruby stopped her.

"Thank you, Abby, I would rather do that myself." She looked around for a clock but didn't see one. "Please knock on my door at a quarter to eight so that I don't keep my aunt waiting."

"Yes, miss." The maid bobbed her a curtsey and left.

Alone at last. Ruby sat on the bed. Firm but not too hard. Good. However, the furniture of polished dark oak was overpowering in the small room. A small escritoire was tucked into one corner. A dresser with a washstand on top and a mirror were against the far wall. She opened the double doors of the large armoire and saw the shelves and hooks for her clothing. Slowly she unpacked her few items of clothing and left the trunk for the maid to take away. With cream coloured walls and dark green curtains on the windows and half tester bed, the effect was almost claustrophobic. It added to her sense of foreboding. Ruby was not sure she could live up to her aunt's expectations. She was in London to please her father, who wanted her to find a good husband, but she took comfort in remembering her own reason for coming – Crispin the dashing botanist. She looked out of the small window to a narrow backyard. At least there was a tree. Its branches had plump green buds. Soon the new leaves would unfurl. She would have a bit of the country to look at here in grey London.

She changed into her second best dress, a pale blue round gown and smoothed her hair. When the maid knocked on her door she was ready to go downstairs. She longed for something to eat. Ruby entered the drawing room. Her Aunt Ada looked up, inspected Ruby's dress and shook her head. "I'm glad you're prompt, child. I can't abide tardiness. But is that what you would wear to dinner with your father?"

"Yes, aunt. It is what I'd wear at home. If I were invited to a friend's for dinner, I would wear a more formal gown."

"I see you have a lot to learn. Once Mme. Faure, my modiste, has created your new wardrobe I will advise you what to wear for each occasion."

"She is a seamstress?" Ruby asked.

"Yes, but she is called a modiste."

When the butler announced that dinner was served, Ruby jumped to her feet eagerly.

"No, no, Ruby. Sit down again. Now rise gracefully to your feet and follow me out of the room. I take precedence over you. At a formal dinner couples walk into the dining room in order of their rank."

They sat down at the dining room table and the butler served them a clear soup. Ruby tried to eat slowly but she was so hungry that she finished well before her aunt. As the next course was served her aunt looked approvingly at her.

"I'm happy to see that you have nice table manners but you must learn to eat more slowly."

Ruby started to smile at the small compliment, then stopped when the rest of her aunt's comment registered.

"Now we must discuss what we will say about your background."

"You mean about my mother?" Ruby said, feeling defensive. She had loved her mother and missed her still.

"Yes. It's best if you don't mention her – er – status."

Ruby's eyes began to flood with tears and she fought to keep her voice from rising in a squeak. "She was a cook but my parents were happy together." She sniffed back another tear.

"That may very well be true, however, if you wish to make a good match it will do you no good to tell anyone about it. Your father is Lord Roderick of Thorncroft Hall in Kent. Your mother died when you were a child. That's all they need to know. If pressed for details say that your mother preferred country life."

"I see," Ruby said. Her friend, Penelope, had advised the very same thing. She hated to think of her sweet mother treated like dirty linen by the ton. Did she even want to be part of this society?

Chapter Two

The next day Ruby put on her old carriage gown and got into Aunt Ada's coach for her first appointment with Mme. Faure.

"Lady Gillingham, what a pleasure to see you and this must be your niece," said an older lady dressed in a very stylish grey silk dress with a lace collar and cuffs.

"Yes. Ruby arrived yesterday and is in dire need of your assistance."

Mme. Faure nodded. "Of course, please do come into the back and I will have some measurements taken. What a lovely fresh complexion you have, young lady."

Ruby followed her to a curtained off area and removed her carriage dress. She stood in her petticoat as Mme. Faure's maid measured her very carefully then helped her back into her clothes. She found her aunt in the front, busy choosing a whole new wardrobe for her, more dresses and gowns than she had ever owned. Aunt Ada ordered morning gowns in pastel coloured gingham and cambric dresses with embroidery, frills and tucks, a new walking gown and a carriage dress.

"You need to have clothes for your dance classes, which must start as soon as possible, and dresses to wear in the evenings. White muslin with these coloured sashes will be most suitable for the dinners you will be attending with the addition of a pelisse to wear over them, of course. You don't need ball gowns until you learn to dance but you will need slippers and a bonnet."

Before Ruby had time to gather her wits, her aunt arranged for some of the clothes to be sent as soon as possible, bid goodbye to Mme. Faure and briskly whisked her out of the shop into the cobbled street. Bruton Street was a very fashionable address although Ruby had no inkling of this fact. She wondered at the strange metal structures on the street corners. What could they be? She had never seen their like in the countryside.

"Those are gaslights, child. At dusk the lamplighters come up the street and light them one at a time. You will see them when we go out to dinner of an evening," her aunt said.

Next, they stopped at a milliners, where Ruby chose a white chip bonnet and flowers so that she could trim it herself. At the shoemaker's shop, her aunt ordered some walking shoes and slippers for dancing.

Eventually when they arrived back at Crescent Street, her aunt's town house, the butler greeted them with a concerned expression on his face. "My lady I'm sorry but Lady Dainsbury is waiting for you in the drawing room. I told her you were not at home but she said it was urgent and insisted on waiting."

"Very well, Jarvis, but I'm not at home to anyone else. Is that clear?"

"Yes, milady, of course. I do apologise."

"Camilla Dainsbury is an old friend of mine but I do

wish she hadn't chosen today to visit." Aunt Ada whispered as she turned to Ruby. "However, it can't be helped. So come along, watch your posture and be careful what you say."

"Yes, aunt, but I could wait in my room until she leaves if you prefer."

"No. Then she would think I was hiding you. I'm sure it's you she wants to see."

Ruby followed her aunt into the room being careful to move slowly and keep her back straight, as she had been taught in boarding school. A very round woman, her aunt's age, dressed in brown and orange plaid taffeta sat on a settee. Her hair looked as if she'd dyed it with henna; it didn't quite cover the grey.

"Ada! I made myself at home. I knew you wouldn't mind. I just had to see this niece of yours."

"Yes, Camilla. This is Ruby Gillingham, my niece. As you will recall her father is my brother, Lord Roderick of Thorncroft Hall in Kent."

Ruby curtseyed to the woman who was eyeing her with frank curiosity.

"Yes, yes. I know all that, Ada. Come here child and sit beside me so we can talk."

Ruby did as she was told, wondering what she was in for.

"Now tell me. Do you have any brothers or sisters, child?"

"I have one half-brother, Matthew, who is at Cambridge, but no sisters."

"And why is he your half-brother?"

"His mother died and then my father married my mother"

"And who is your mother, dear?"

Ruby shot a glance at her aunt before replying but there was no help coming from that quarter. "My mother died when I was twelve. She was Mistress Violet Jennings before she married my father. She preferred country life to the city –"

"— That's enough, Camilla," her aunt cut in. "Must you interrogate the poor girl on her first day in London? Now, tell me, how is Cassandra? Last I remember, she was enjoying her dance classes."

"Oh, yes, Cassandra loves dancing and Monsieur Richard is such a wonderful instructor. He says that my granddaughter is the best pupil he's ever had." Lady Dainsbury beamed with pride.

"Ruby needs dancing lessons. I will contact this M. Richard."

"I highly recommend him and you can tell him I said so. Now, I must take my leave. It was very interesting to meet you, Ruby. Goodbye Ada, my dear." And with a swirl of plaid taffeta she waddled out of the drawing room.

***

A few days later Ruby found herself in M. Richard's dance studio wearing an apple green cambric gown and her new dancing slippers, which pinched.

"Ah. Miss Gillingham? The young lady recommended to me by Lady Dainsbury." He bowed to her and her aunt.

"Yes, sir. I am Ruby Gillingham," she said bobbing a curtsey.

"Very good. Please take your place in line with the other jeune filles. Today we are practicing the cotillion which is similar to one of your English country dances."

For the next hour Ruby and a dozen other girls practiced the ten different figures that would be performed within the square formation of the cotillion. When M. Richard was satisfied that the girls understood the patterns he chose eight of them to make up one set. To her amazement Ruby was one of the jeunes filles selected. She tried her best to remember the sequence of changes but everything was so new, she became ended up very confused.

"Stop!" called out M. Richard. "You," he said pointing to Ruby, "need to observe. Then it will become clear to you. Cassandra, take her place." Then he turned to Ruby again. "Watch this demoiselle. She knows the steps tres bien."

Ruby did as directed. She stood to the side of the room and watched. Yes. Cassandra moved with graceful steps, always on the beat and seemed to be thoroughly enjoying herself. Ruby sighed. It would be lovely to be able to dance like that. When the girls stopped to rest, Cassandra came over to her.

"Hello. I'm Cassandra Dainsbury. My grandmother told me you had just come to London. Isn't it amazing? All the shops and so many people and such beautiful clothes."

"I haven't been anywhere excepting my aunt's dressmaker, or rather, her modiste."

Cassandra smiled, "Yes. I'm trying to learn all the French names too."

"Where are you from?" Ruby asked examining the petite blonde.

"I'm from Yorkshire but I've been staying with my grandmamma for a year now to pick up some town bronze." At Ruby's puzzled expression she explained, "So that I don't act like a country bumpkin."

"You dance so well," Ruby said. "I hope I can learn quickly."

"You will. It's fun isn't it? And M. Richard is so handsome." She giggled.

Ruby looked at the dance instructor again. Handsome? Not in her opinion but then she compared every man to Crispin, Lord Sayward, who was the epitome of handsome with his tall manly figure and deep set grey eyes which seemed to caress her with every glance.Richard called them back to class and they repeated the figures. This time Ruby made fewer mistakes. At the end of class he announced, "Merci, mes demoiselles. Next week we progress to the quadrille."

As Ruby travelled home in her aunt's carriage she got a whiff of the garbage strewn streets. She looked out at the houses that were crowded close together on either side, not a tree was in sight. What a difference this was to driving her tilbury through the green meadows of Kent. She remembered the canopy of little white blossoms over her head and the linden tree's heavenly scent. It had enveloped her on her ride back to Thorncroft after Berrington had rescued her from a dipping. The memory filled her with longing but her aunt broke her concentration.

"You have some catching up to do because the class started a month ago but I think you did fairly well, Ruby. Dancing takes practice."

When they arrived at Crescent Street, a letter was waiting for Ruby from her friend, Penelope. Eagerly, she tore open the seal and read it very quickly, then settled down to re-read it a second time. What was it that Penelope had written about Crispin? He had been ill with a high fever from some tropical disease but was now recovering. Thank goodness. He had to come back to England by autumn. He just had to. She crossed her fingers.

She could not wait to reply. "Aunt, please may I have

a piece of stationery as I promised to write to my friend, Penelope, every week."

"Yes, child. Go to the library and open the top left drawer of my desk. Take one piece of paper from there. You don't want your friend to have to pay too much postage."

"Thank you, aunt, I always write across the page as well as down if necessary." Her aunt nodded approvingly.

Ruby went into the library. Unlike other rooms in the town house it seemed a very masculine domain with brown velvet drapes covering the windows and a big leather covered armchair behind a dark walnut desk. It appeared that her aunt hadn't changed anything since she became a widow many years ago. She found the paper in the drawer but as she turned to leave she noticed the life-sized painting hanging above the fireplace and stopped. It was of two small children, a girl and a boy. The boy seemed the older. He wore a sailor suit and held a hoop in one hand and a stick in the other. The girl was little more than a toddler dressed in a lacy white dress. She stared out of the painting with a puzzled expression. But Ruby was drawn back to the boy's face, there was something familiar about his expression. Then it dawned on her. It was likely her father and Ada as children. She remained staring at the portrait until a maid came looking for her.

"Miss, her ladyship wishes to see you in the drawing room," she said.

When Ruby arrived she couldn't wait to have her suspicions confirmed. "I was admiring the painting in the library. It's my father as a child isn't it? And the little girl – is she you?"

"Yes, that is your father but not myself. That was our

sister, Sophie, who died of scarlet fever when she was barely two. I was born later."

"I'm sorry about your sister, aunt. But my father still has that expression when he's showing off something he's proud of, like a new colt or a phaeton."

Her aunt nodded absently, "Yes, yes. I'm sure you're right. Now, we will be at home to callers this afternoon so put on your tucked gingham afternoon dress and have the maid redo your hair. Be back here no later than two o'clock."

"Yes, aunt," Ruby said then she hurried to her room so that she could write her letter first.

She sat at the little escritoire and sharpened a goose quill before dipping it into the inkwell, paused, then wrote.

Dear Penelope,

Where to begin? My life here is so different than at home. Aunt is kind enough but is constantly finding fault with me. I walk too fast, I eat too fast, I eat too much. I'm not accomplished enough. But I've started dance classes and there is one girl, Cassandra, who seems nice. Her grandmother is a friend of Aunt Ada's so I'll likely see more of her.

Just before I left home I had a strange encounter I haven't had a chance to tell you about. I had taken Poppy down that avenue of Linden trees you know I love. I decided to pick some blossoms and slipped on the wet ground, twisting my ankle. I hobbled to the pond to soak my sore foot and a man appeared. He was very good looking with vivid blue eyes and pleasing features. He had just arrived from Ireland, and said he had inherited Linden Hall. His name is Peter, Lord Berrington. He teased me about my beautiful feet, carried me up to my tilbury, as if I weighed no more than a feather, and drove me home. I'm sorry I didn't get a chance to get to know him better. There was something very appealing about him – but nothing like Crispin of course.

I'm worried about Crispin. I do hope he's all right. As you know I'm hoping he'll be back in England in time for the Little Season in September. Aunt thinks I may be up to scratch by then.

I miss you and I miss Thorncroft Hall as well as the green fields and gardens of Kent. Write soon,

Your friend,

Ruby

P.S. I'm sorry this may be hard to read since there was so much to say I had to write across the page as well as down.

***

The maid laced up the corset over Ruby's chemise and dropped her new white muslin dinner gown over her shoulders. It fell with gossamer softness to the floor. If Ruby hadn't been so stressed by the prospect of her first formal dinner party she would have enjoyed the sensation more. The maid arranged the long ends of her blue velvet sash around her cinched in waist and tied the ends into little bows.

"There," she said with a smile. "You look a treat, miss."

"Thank you, Abby, If only I wasn't so nervous. How will I be able to eat anything with my corset tied so tightly?"

"Just take little tastes, miss, don't even try to clean your plate."

Ruby mulled this over and decided she'd be too nervous to have much appetite anyway. Maybe she could have some bread and cheese when they returned? When her hair was done, complete with a little white rosebud tucked into the chignon, she walked slowly downstairs for her aunt's inspection.

"Yes, child. You'll do. Now we must be off. Put on your pelisse."

As the butler placed the evening cloak around her shoulders Ruby felt the softness of fine wool envelope her. She loved her new clothes.

As the carriage pulled away Aunt Ada began explaining whom she would meet that evening. "Lord Trafferton will be there. He's quite tall so he won't mind your height. He has a nice estate in Sussex but he does tend to go on about his hunting dogs. Being from the country you might not mind that."

Ruby suppressed a qualm and tried to look cheerful.

"Matilda, Lady Sarne, is our hostess and her two daughters will also be in attendance. She will see you as competition for them but Lord Sarne is a kindly man. If you're lucky he'll take you in to dinner. I think the Trenton brothers will be present and you can expect attention from both of them. The eldest, James, takes precedence over his brother, Stephen. But the Sarnes will go in to dinner first because their title is the oldest."

"Aunt, how will I ever keep all this straight in my head?"

"For tonight you don't have to. Just hold back when dinner is announced and someone will offer you his arm. Smile, thank them and take it. And remember to watch your hostess for cues so you'll know when it is time to turn and speak with the person on your left."

When they arrived at the home of Lord and Lady Sarne, Aunt Ada introduced Ruby as her niece from Kent. Lady Sarne introduced her two daughters and as she let them lead Ruby away her heart sank. They were the same two girls from the Ladies' Seminary whom she had secretly dubbed the wicked stepsisters. Lettice, the tall, thin one looked Ruby over from head to foot with a gleam in her eye whilst Fleur seemed fascinated by a marble statue of the three graces.

"You have a new dress and it's even in style," she said giggling. She glanced over at her sister. "Did you notice, Fleur?" She chortled again as if she had made a good joke.

"Your aunt has a good modiste. It suits you," Fleur said. She had always been the kinder of the two but had always backed up her sister.

"At the Ladies' Seminary you looked as if your mother had made all your clothes," Lettice continued daring Ruby to incriminate herself.

"My mother was not a seamstress," Ruby said her voice barely above a whisper. Her eyes began to smart with unshed tears. This was exactly why she hadn't wanted to come to London. She turned her back on the girls but moved too hastily and bumped into a man standing behind her.

"I'm so sorry," she said looking up into a kindly older man's face. It was her host. Now she really wanted to sink through the floor.

"Don't apologize, my dear. No harm done. I wasn't holding anything I could spill," he smiled. "You're Lady Paxton's niece. I've forgotten your name already. I'm the one who should apologize."

"It's Ruby, milord. Ruby Gillingham." Thank goodness she'd bumped into him rather than someone else. She took a deep breath and let it out.

"You must be finding London quite a change from the country," he said.

"Very much so, milord. I'm not used to so many people."

"You're from Kent?" he paused. "Ah, I remember. Thorncroft Hall. Your father has quite the stable."

"Horses are his whole world, milord."

"And what about you, young lady? What do you do?"

"I sing and I like to draw. But I'm very interested in

the new glasshouses. My neighbours have one and it's fascinating to see what they can grow now."

"Yes. They're the latest thing these conservatories. You should talk to Trafferton over there. He's in the process of building one." He took her arm and walked her over to him.

"Trafferton, I would like you to meet Miss Gillingham from Kent." The young man bowed to her and she bobbed a curtsey. "She has an interest in glasshouses," Lord Sarne said, before moving on to speak to his other guests.

Lord Trafferton had a friendly face and a thick mop of curly brown hair. Ruby decided he wasn't too intimidating and at least they had a common interest. "Lord Sarne said that you're building a conservatory. Is that so, milord?"

"Yes, at Tadcomb Hall in Sussex. It should be completed by the end of the summer."

"My neighbours in Kent have one and grow the most amazing orchids. What are you planning to cultivate?"

"Pineapples, mostly."

"Pineapples? They're a tropical fruit I know. But I've never seen one. What do they taste like?"

"Very sweet, usually, but they can be quite acidic and strong tasting. You may see one at a dinner party before long." Another young man wandered over to join them. "Now James, here, wants to grow tropical water lilies."

James Trenton bowed as Trafferton introduced Ruby. He had a short, delicate build and wore a brightly coloured vest.

"You find glass houses interesting? How unusual. Most young ladies are only interested in the flowers grown in them," Trenton said.

"I like flowers also but I'd be more interested in growing

strawberries in January. Do you think that would that be possible?" Ruby asked.

"I don't know," Trenton replied. "It depends on their natural growing cycle."

"Exactly," Trafferton cut in. "You see pineapples grow all year round, not so strawberries."

When dinner was announced, Ruby remembered her aunt's advice. She held back as instructed and waited to be invited. She looked over the heads of the guests for a few moments and then heard someone clearing their throat. It was Trafferton.

"May I have the pleasure of escorting you in to dinner, Miss Gillingham?"

"Why, thank you, milord," Ruby said as she took his arm. She noticed that Lettice was glaring at her. What now? Perhaps she had a secret tendre for Trafferton? Ruby stole another glance at him and decided he was definitely one of the more attractive young men present. Lettice herself was on the arm of James, with the colourful vest and she towered above him.

"How big is your conservatory, milord?" she asked Lord Trafferton.

"Hmm...about the size of Lady Sarne's drawing room I would say. When it's finished I plan to hold a small reception to show it off. I'll make sure you receive an invitation."

"Thank you, milord that would be most kind." Ruby beamed at him. "Why did you decide to build a conservatory, if you don't mind me asking?" He seemed surprised by her question.

"Well, it's the latest thing. I like to be part of new inventions, don't you know? Not the same old, same old."

"So it's not an ardent interest in botany?"

"Heavens no. Hardly know one plant from another, but I've hired a good gardener to see to that."

"I see. I have a friend in Kent who just inherited an old estate and is interested in building a glasshouse. I was hoping you could tell me how it works. How it's heated in the winter. That sort of thing."

"Don't know. But you can find out when you come to see it."

As dinner was served Ruby remembered just to take little bites but it did seem such a waste of good food. She had a few spoonfuls of a clear soup only to have it whisked away as removes of various fish dishes arrived on the table in two rows. She had a taste of turbot in a cream sauce and some salmon. The eels and smelts she happily ignored. When the goose and haunch of venison arrived she felt she couldn't eat another bite even though the accompanying asparagus and French beans looked very appetizing. Thankfully, she realized that she could still breathe comfortably despite her tight corset and she refocused on the conversation around her. Lady Sarne had turned to the guest on her left so Ruby did likewise. Trenton, of the colourful vest, smiled politely at her. "Is this your first visit to London, Miss Gillingham?" he asked.

"Yes. I'm quite overwhelmed by it, actually. It seems to me that Londoners barely sleep and that the street vendors never do."

"Oh yes, but one gets used to it and I find it quite stimulating. There are all the musical events, as well as opera, the theater and dances, not to mention the exhibits and lectures."

"I would love to attend the opera or go to the theatre but

I haven't had the opportunity yet. Do you live here all year round, milord?"

"Oh no, just for the Season and sometimes the Little Season as well. The rest of the time I go to our estate in the Lake District."

"I've heard its lovely there." Ruby said.

"Yes, when it doesn't rain, that is." He smiled ruefully.

Just then dessert was served. The butlers brought in an impressive array of dishes. Ruby decided to try the towering croque-en-bouche covered in a chocolate glaze because it was filled with a cream made with pineapple. She had a small portion of the refreshing lemon gelee, too. There was also a multi-layered hazelnut cake and some darling apricot soufflés but Ruby couldn't swallow another mouthful. Then she noticed something taking pride of place in the middle of the table.

"Milord," she said, turning back to Trafferton, "Is that a pineapple?"

"Yes. It is but, take my advice. Don't ask for a slice." When he saw her puzzled expression he said in a low whisper. "It's likely rented." Then he turned away to speak with the lady on his left. Ruby decided that she would have to ask Aunt Ada what he meant later.

Chapter Three

Soon it was time for the ladies to withdraw so the gentlemen could have their port and cigars in peace. As she made her way to the drawing room, Ruby made a point of avoiding the Sarne girls, the wicked stepsisters and noticed a young woman who was already seated on a settee near the hearth. She was alone.

"Good evening. May I join you? I don't believe we've met. I'm Ruby Gillingham," she said with a smile. The girl turned to her eagerly.

"I'm so happy to meet you. I don't know anyone here except my godmother. Caitlin Trigan's my name."

"Are you from Ireland?" Ruby asked.

"How did you know?" Caitlin replied in surprise.

"It's the lovely lilt in your speech. Recently I met a man who spoke as you do. He's a new neighbour of ours, in Kent. Peter, Lord Berrington."

"My brother's name is Peter and I know he just came into a title but I don't remember what it is. I do hope he comes to London to visit soon. I would love his company."

"Perhaps you could write him a letter? I correspond with

my best friend every week and it doesn't take very long to get a reply."

"What a good idea but I'm afraid I don't know how to contact him."

"If it's this Lord Berrington, I can give you the address because he's almost our neighbour."

"You can? I'd appreciate that very much," Caitlin said with surprise.

"Are you here to prepare for the Little Season too?" Ruby asked.

"Yes. I think that's the plan. My godmother thinks it's time to find a husband but I'm not sure I want to marry quite yet. I'm not ready to settle down and have a baby every year. I play the harp and I want to focus on my music and take lessons from the best teachers. But Lady Sally, my godmother, thinks that's a silly notion. She says you can play the harp at any stage of your life but now is the time to marry. What about you?"

"I do want a home of my own but I wouldn't want to marry just anyone. Right now though, I'm struggling to catch up on the dance classes my aunt enrolled me in. Are you taking them too?" Ruby asked.

"Yes, with a M. Richard on Tuesday mornings. He's always talking French to us – as if we should know what he means," Caitlin replied making a little grimace.

"I go to him in the afternoons. Perhaps we could try to get in the same class?" Ruby suggested eagerly but an elegant lady in a deep maroon gown and matching turban came up to them before Caitlin could give an answer. Instead, she said, "Ah here comes Lady Sally. I'll introduce you. Lady Sally I've made a new friend. This is Miss Ruby Gillingham from Kent." Then she turned to Ruby. "This is my godmother, Sally, Lady Dabbley."

"I'm happy to meet you milady," Ruby said bobbing a courtesy.

"Delighted. You must come to tea sometime soon. Caitlin needs friends her own age," Lady Dabbley replied.

***

Berrington looked around the crowded ballroom where the cream of London's aristocracy congregated. It still amazed him that he was now a part of it, when only six months ago he was a penniless student at Oxford. But here he was and now he must adapt to life among the ton. Arriving late the night before, he had stayed at a posting inn rather than calling on his sister's godparents who would certainly have asked him to stay. However, he'd decided against doing so as he preferred his attendance tonight to be a surprise for Caitlin. She had penned him a letter, full of excited details about this ball. Perhaps that pretty Miss Gillingham with hair the colour of chestnuts in the autumn would also be among the throng? There she was! Dancing with a very serious expression on her face. It looked as if she were trying hard to remember the steps of the cotillion. Berrington smiled to himself. He must show her that dancing was meant to be fun. Now where was Caitlin? Oh, that was easy. Her red hair stood out in a sea of blonde, black and the old-fashioned powdered wigs.

It was September, the beginning of the Little Season and Aunt Ada had declared that Ruby could now participate with the proviso that her dance classes continue. This was Ruby's first ball and Caitlin's, too. The tall beeswax candles made the crystal chandeliers glow and the flickering light picked out the sparkle of jewels worn by the ladies. Their silks and satins rustled when they moved through the grandly decorated ballroom.

Spicy perfumes mingled in the night air adding to the magic of the evening. Ruby gazed in awe.

"Oh look! There's Peter, my brother," Caitlin cried.

Ruby watched as Peter, Lord Berrington, wove his way toward them through the crowd. His skin had a healthy outdoor glow and his simple black and white evening clothes made him stand out against the pale-faced gentlemen dressed in fancy brocades and laces. Many had added padding inside their clothing, so as to appear well built, but Berrington needed no such help from his tailor. His muscles were his own. He swept the girls a graceful bow as they curtseyed.

"Peter, it's so good to see you! When did you arrive?" Caitlin asked.

"I arrived yesterday, dear sister. I thought you'd be happy to see a friendly face," he replied. "And Miss Gillingham, I'm pleased to see you looking so well." His gaze swept down to the floor as if to check Ruby's ankle.

"Thank you, milord." Ruby blushed but couldn't help smiling at him. She had forgotten how handsome he was.

"Now which of you lovely ladies will dance with me first? I checked, Caitlin, the next country dance is one we did at home in Ireland."

"In that case, you two should take the floor together." Ruby said.

She stood to one side and watched as Peter led his sister into the crowd of swirling couples. They looked so happy together and did the steps with barely any hesitation. When the dance ended she met them by the refreshment stand.

"May I have the pleasure of a dance, later this evening?" Berrington asked Ruby, then qualified his request by adding, "Although I'm not sure which ones I can do."

"Yes, thank you," Ruby said as she wrote his name in her dance card. "But you may have to wait a little while."

"I don't mind. Are you enjoying your stay in London?"

"Some of it, like tonight, is very pleasant but I miss Kent. London is never quiet enough for me."

"I know what you mean. It's like a beehive," Berrington said.

Ruby giggled then looked down, trying to compose herself. She noticed a pair of polished men's boots right in front of her. She raised her eyes only to find Crispin, Lord Sayward standing before her.

"Miss Gillingham. What a surprise," he said bowing.

He was here at last! Her heart began to beat faster as she looked into his beautiful grey eyes. He was tanned and taller than she remembered. She had to force herself not to reach out and touch him. She knew she was staring.

"Would you do me the honour of the next dance, Miss Gillingham?" he asked.

"Why thank you," she said as her stomach did a somersault. It was a quadrille. Could she remember how to do it? Then, she remembered that it was similar to a cotillion and she knew the general pattern of that after all the practice at M. Richard's. But she hoped she would be able to do the 'figures' between each set that made it different. Mentally crossing her fingers, she placed her gloved hand in Lord Sayward's as he led her onto the dance floor.

The music began and she tried to relax. She loved this melody. Ruby navigated the first change without a mishap. But then she made the mistake of looking at Crispin as he smiled at the pretty brunette he was leading around in a figure eight. A bolt of jealousy surged through her. No! That girl couldn't have him. He was her Crispin! Within two steps he was back at her side. As his fingers clasped hers, her mind went blank. What was she supposed to do next? Crispin waited patiently as they missed their turn and Ruby felt a hot flush creeping over her face. She managed to finish the dance correctly but felt thoroughly mortified.

"I'm so sorry milord," Ruby began but Crispin held up his hand.

"Think nothing of it. I did the same myself when I first came to town. It's been my pleasure, Miss Gillingham." He bowed and disappeared into the crowd.

Ruby watched Caitlin dance a cotillion with a gentleman who was a little shorter than her and then realized it was James Trenton, of the coloured vest. Today he wore the required white waistcoat with an artfully tied neck cloth and satin knee breeches.

It was almost time for the midnight supper when Berrington bowed before her once again.

"I believe I have the honour of the next dance," he stated.

"Yes, milord, a quadrille," Ruby answered bobbing him a curtsey. She felt more confident on the dance floor now but still she focused very carefully on the sequence of steps. Berrington, however, seemed completely at ease. At one point when she hesitated he whispered "chase me" in her ear. Oh yes. That jogged her memory to the French, "chasse". She followed him in the intricate manoeuver and ended up exactly where she was meant to be.

"That was rather fun," Ruby admitted when the dance ended.

"And you did very well," he replied.

"Only with your help. Thank you."

"It was my pleasure, Miss Gillingham. We must do this again sometime."

"Will you be staying long in town?"

"I'm not sure, actually. Linden Hall requires furnishing, and I have not found what I'm looking for yet."

The rest of the evening flew by in a flurry and about two in the morning, Ruby climbed into the carriage, with a jumble of dance steps still in her head. Aunt Ada was very curious about her dance partners.

"You danced three times tonight, one of which was Lord Trafferton but who were the other two gentlemen?"

"The first was Lord Sayward. I met him at my neighbour's in Kent before he went off to Haiti for six months. He's interested in conservatories." Ruby answered.

"Hmm... You seemed very flustered whilst dancing with him. Perhaps that is to be expected, it was your first dance after all. Lord Sayward would certainly be quite a catch... if you could get past his mother. She's a bit of a dragon."

That wasn't why she had blushed and lost her place in the dance and she knew it, but Ruby could never admit that to her aunt. The new tidbit of information about Crispin's mother didn't sound promising though.

"With whom did you dance the cotillion, just before supper?" her aunt wanted to know.

"That was Peter, Lord Berrington. He just came into an estate near ours in Kent, called Linden Hall."

"But how is it you know his first name?"

"I was out for a drive in father's new tilbury. I dismounted to pick some flowers and I twisted my ankle. He helped me get home."

"You were out – all by yourself?" her aunt asked with raised eyebrows.

"Yes, of course. It's very close to Thornton. I go everywhere by myself."

"That's very improper. Clearly, things are different out in the countryside. Now we must focus on finding you just the right husband," her aunt said as they alighted from the carriage and went indoors.

"Come into the drawing room. We'll have a tisane before bed," her aunt said.

"Why is it so important that I make a good marriage?" Ruby asked making herself comfortable on a settee by the hearth where a fire blazed.

"It's for your own happiness and comfort," her aunt replied. "Surely you can see that being able to have your own carriage and enough servants to make a house run smoothly is something to be desired?"

Ruby nodded, albeit rather hesitantly.

"And I'd love to have you living near me in London, or no further than the outskirts. Then when you set up your nursery I'll be able to come and play with your little ones," her aunt said as a wistful look crossed her face. "I never had any children and always longed to hold my own in my arms. Yours would still be my flesh and blood. It would be a dream come true."

Ruby saw the longing on her aunt's face and her heart opened. "Aunt, I promise that when I have babies you can come and play with them as much as you like." They smiled at each other. "But I must be honest with you. I'm not sure that I want to live in London, I do miss the countryside so."

"That's why I said, perhaps on the outskirts. Of course it all depends on the man you marry doesn't it? First things first. I've had my eye on a Mr. Fenwick. He has a tidy fortune and a house about half an hour outside the city."

"Oh? What is he like?" Ruby asked.

"He's nice looking, in his late thirties, a widower with no children and he likes music. Oh yes, and he has an interest in those glasshouses your Mr. Greenley is involved in."

"I see," Ruby replied. "When am I going to meet him?" Obviously, her aunt had carefully laid plans in place but at least she was honest about it.

"You'll meet him this Thursday at Lady Malmsby's garden party. Mr. Fenwick wouldn't miss it."

"I look forward to it," Ruby said with apprehension. "By the way aunt, I've been meaning to ask you about something Lord Trafferton said at dinner the other evening. There was a pineapple on the table and he said to take his advice and not ask for a slice because it was likely rented?"

"Oh yes. I don't know if Lady Sarne rented that one, but frequently it is done, just to use as a table centre. After the dinner it is returned to the caterer. Of course if a guest asks for a slice it must be cut. Once cut, the hostess must pay for it. Lord Trafferton gave you good advice for one never knows how old a rented pineapple may be."

Ruby just shook her head in disbelief. The ton certainly had some strange customs. She would never think of putting anything on the dinner table that a guest couldn't eat.

***

The next day two bouquets arrived. The first was a pretty arrangement of yellow mullein and white carnations from Crispin. The note read, "To my charming dance partner, until we meet again, Sayward."

"How lovely. White carnations mean 'sweet and lovely'

and mullein means 'courage'," Aunt Ada explained with a nod of approval. "Very appropriate." While Ruby was examining the second bouquet of pink and white flowers, looking for the note she continued, "Now, let's see. That one is very different. Stocks mean 'you will always be beautiful to me' and Queen Anne's lace stands for 'fantasy'. What does the note say?"

Ruby read it out to her, "Since I can't send you Linden blossoms I hope you'll enjoy these too, Berrington."

"I should think not." Her aunt looked scandalized. "It would have been very inappropriate for him to send Linden blossoms to you – even if they were in season."

"Why? Whatever do you mean, aunt?" Ruby was puzzled.

"Linden blossoms stand for 'conjugal love'," she said shaking her head. "Ruby, I do believe you have made an impression on both gentlemen."

Chapter Four

∞

Ruby took a deep breath as she and her aunt arrived at Lady Malmsby's town house. She hated the idea that Aunt Ada had such high expectations for this first meeting with Mr. Fenwick. Once inside, she relaxed a little. Lady Malmsby's elaborately designed garden was simply stunning. Hedges camouflaged the brick walls that surrounded the unusually large city plot and artfully muffled the city noise. Wrought iron benches were arranged around the perimeter, tucked away under climbing rose arbours. Yet more late-blooming roses of every colour were laid out in formal beds interspersed with clipped boxwood shrubs. Amidst these roses, a statue of a Grecian woman in elegant draperies topped a fountain in which the water tinkled softly. Ruby sighed with pleasure. To find a green oasis like this in the heart of London made her country heart rejoice. The guests inspected the flowers and then sat at little tables under white canvas umbrellas sipping tea and eating cucumber sandwiches, for the autumn sun could still be quite hot.

When Aunt Ada introduced Mr. Fenwick, Ruby's heart

sank. Her aunt had been correct. He was nice looking but compared to Crispin, or even Berrington, he seemed as bland as a milk pudding. She took a deep breath knowing she must talk to him for her aunt's sake.

"I love to be out of doors," she said. "And it's hard to do in the city."

"I know what you mean," he replied. "One can walk in Hyde Park but it's not the same as the open countryside." Then as if he couldn't believe he had revealed so much about himself, he blushed. He pointed to a small Michaelmas daisy just coming into blossom. "These grow in profusion on my estate."

Ruby found him pleasant enough and were he to ask her to go for a walk, she might consider it. But if Crispin suggested the same? She smiled. She would jump up and ask, "When? Where?" And what if Berrington were to ask, as well? Yes, she decided with a smile, walking with him would be a pleasure also. Did she want to live in London? Definitely not, but most of the aristocracy had country estates and only spent part of the year in the bustling city. Crispin came to mind at once. His estate of Rowangate in Wiltshire would be just perfect. Of course he was her first choice but she must be realistic. She might not be acceptable in his world.

Berrington made her laugh but would her father approve of him? Perhaps the perfect man would appear at the next ball? She shook her head at her own foolishness. From what she had seen so far, there weren't very many handsome, young peers-of-the-realm. And even Aunt Ada seemed oblivious to that fact. The first thing she mentioned about a man was his financial status and then his age. There did seem to be a lot of widowers hoping to re-marry and much to Ruby's dismay, her aunt seemed to know many of them.

***

Caitlin had managed to rearrange her dance class with M. Richard so that from now on she could practice with both Ruby and Cassandra. The focus of their lesson this week was to learn the rudiments of 'the waltz'. The room was buzzing with excitement because it was considered quite scandalous to have a stranger hold you so intimately in his arms as you danced.

"Mes desmoiselles," M. Richard raised his voice to get their attention. "As you know, the waltz has been popular since Tsar Alexander first danced it at Almacks in 1814. As debutantes although you will need permission to perform this dance, it is best that you become well acquainted with the steps. I will demonstrate. Observe closely." He held out his hand to Cassandra who stepped forward. M. Richard took her in his arms and gasps filled the room. "Music. Please."

Miss Timmins began to play a waltz as M. Richard led Cassandra in a slow circle to three quarter time. How would it feel to have Crispin hold her like that? Ruby was brought back to earth as the lilting music stopped and M. Richard began to speak again.

"You have just witnessed the waltz in full dance position but you will be learning a modified version, the open waltz position. "First we will have half of you take the man's part and then later you will change roles."

"I'll be the man, first," Caitlin said to Ruby as they paired up. "I've danced like this with my brother."

"First the lady places her left hand on the gentleman's right shoulder as they both face in the same direction which is called the line of dance. Please do so. Bien. Now they clasp their other hands in front. Practice holding this position as you dance the waltz step. One, two, three. One, two, three. Now, the lady slides her left hand down behind her waist and the man clasps her hand just so. Then they turn to face each other." M. Richard hurried around the room correcting hand and body positions to his satisfaction. There was a lot of giggling as the girls tried to follow his instructions.

"Ow! You stepped on my foot," yelped a plump girl with a perpetual scowl on her face.

"Stop!" their teacher ordered. "I can see that you will all require much practice to learn this dance correctly. Ladies! Please calm down. How are you going to dance with a gentleman if you cannot do this simple step with another jeune fille?"

Over the next few weeks they slowly learned how to waltz around the room in open position. The turns took more practice but eventually they could all spin around the dance studio in time to the music. Ruby felt confident that she could do it on the dance floor, if asked, but doubted that she would be given permission to try it.

***

As the days passed Ruby felt more at home living in the city and she knew that Ada enjoyed launching her niece into society. However, she wished that she herself felt more confident for the prospect of endless afternoon teas and soirees was still rather daunting.

"The Pennington's Ball is four days off and you will need a fitting for your new gown," her aunt said. "We will go right after luncheon."

Mme. Faure's face lit up with pleasure when they arrived at her shop. "I am so happy to see you today!" she exclaimed. "Your gown is ready but I hope we do not have to make many alterations as we are very busy with ladies preparing for the Pennington's Ball."

When Ruby tried on the dress the only adjustment needed was a tiny tuck at the Empire waist. Her aunt would be pleased; she was becoming the lady everyone here in the ton expected, well at least on the outside. If only she didn't feel like such an imposter. It was simply not in her to prevaricate if questioned about her mother. But when Ruby looked in the mirror she felt as if Cinderella's godmother had waved a magic wand. The dress was a lovely confection of gauze over satin in the palest blush pink, which Ruby knew flattered her complexion. She had satin slippers dyed to match. Heaven!

The morning of the dance her aunt looked quite excited. "The Pennington's Ball is sure to be a crush. We likely won't get home till dawn so do try to get a little rest this afternoon. I'm sure at least one of your admirers will be there." She smiled as she handed Ruby a small jewellery case. "I thought you might borrow my amethysts this evening."

"Thank you, aunt, how kind. I have very little jewellery except for my Mother's pearl earrings." She opened the blue velvet case to find a matching set of necklace, bracelet and earrings. The amethysts were fashioned into clusters of violets picked out with tiny diamonds. "How beautiful! I promise to take good care of your jewels."

"They look very well with your dress and your chestnut hair, my dear," her aunt said, as Ruby put on the earrings and fastened the antique gold clasps.

***

Ruby stood to one side of the ballroom watching elegant couples circle the floor in a lovely Viennese waltz. The dancers created a kaleidoscope of colour as they twirled in three quarter time and she was filled with a longing to join them. She had partnered Trafferton in a cotillion earlier and managed it without any mishaps but this dance fascinated her.

"It looks like fun doesn't it?" A deep voice whispered at her shoulder. She turned to find Berrington standing closely beside her.

"Yes, but I doubt that my aunt would ever give me permission," Ruby sighed.

"We could dance out on the back terrace where no one will see us," he suggested with a persuasive look. Ruby's pulse began to race.

"How do you know about a back terrace?" She asked feeling as though she was treading on thin ice.

"It's right next to the study where gentlemen go to smoke cigars. And don't worry, they're too busy drinking port to look out of the windows."

"Well, if you're sure." She really shouldn't do this but she would love to actually dance the waltz herself. "How do I get there?"

"Now that's the easy part," he said. "You go down the hall, past the ladies' retiring room, turn left and go out the door at the end of the hall. I'll be waiting outside. But hurry. They're just tuning up."

Ruby did as he had instructed and soon found herself on the empty moonlit terrace. Where was he? A dark figure stepped out of the shadows. Ruby gasped. Berrington looked different somehow, more masculine and even a little seductive.

"May I have the honour of this dance, Miss Gillingham?" he asked bowing deeply.

"Yes, milord," Ruby flashed him a smile as she bobbed

a curtsey. She could hear the violins softly playing the opening bars of her favourite waltz. This felt like a dream..

"If we do the full dance position it will be much easier, all right?" he asked.

Ruby nodded. This was so daring. She knew her aunt would disapprove but she wanted to know how to do the waltz properly, not just the modified, open position. Berrington took her in his arms and Ruby felt her pulse pick up. She could feel his muscular arms holding her and suddenly felt small, petite even. How odd. Being taller than most of the women of her acquaintance that was not how she normally thought of herself. The waltz music drifted out over the night air. She could hear him humming softly along with it. How nice.

Then he stepped forward, right on her foot! She squeaked and he chuckled. She had forgotten all her practicing, he had moved and she had just stood still. He dropped his arms and smiled at her.

"Let's try it again. First I take your right hand in my left hand. Behold. Then I place my right hand, just so." He put his right hand just above Ruby's waist, below her shoulder blades. He was holding her so close. It was shocking but she liked it.

"Now you place your left hand against my right shoulder," he continued. "Your elbow must not collapse as we move forward. If you hold it like this –" Berrington adjusted her hand position. " – You will feel when I am about to step forward, even before I do."

This time Ruby remembered to move her foot and they were off. Berrington kept counting for a few more bars but by then Ruby could move to the beat herself. She loved the sensation of spinning around the terrace together. It felt almost like flying. She was sorry when the music ended.

Berrington kept his arms around her for a moment longer. Then he released her but kept holding her left hand. "I would like to dance with you till dawn," he said bringing her gloved hand to his lips to kiss the back tenderly.

"I would too," she said. "But I must go."

She picked up her skirts and hurried to the door. No one was in sight so she slipped into the ladies retiring room and sat down at a dressing table. She looked at herself in the mirror. Her face was flushed and a few curls had come loose from her chignon. She asked a maid for a glass of water and patted her hair into place. The door opened and Cassandra came in.

"There you are. Your aunt's been looking for you. She seems quite worried."

"I'll go find her, immediately." Ruby answered. At least she'd had a few minutes to catch her breath. That had been risky. What if someone had seen her waltzing on the terrace with Berrington? In full dance position? Would she be compromised? She didn't know how strictly society's rules were enforced. She went into the ballroom to find her aunt talking to other chaperones.

"Ruby, at last! Where were you?"

"I was in the ladies retiring room. I felt a little faint." She fibbed, then whispered, "The maid had to loosen my stays."

"That's all well and good, my dear, but you may have missed a chance to dance with Lord Sayward. He was looking for someone and he walked right past me though I doubt he knows I'm your aunt. Then I think he went into the smoking room down the hall."

Oh dear, what if he had looked out of the windows and seen her with Berrington? But surely he wouldn't tell on her. A few minutes later Lord Fenwick appeared at her side just as they were starting a dance called 'Hole in the wall'. She was happy to have a partner for the simple line dance. Lord Fenton looked to be concentrating very hard but he didn't make any mistakes. When they bowed to each other at the end he seemed visibly relieved.

"Thank you, Miss Gillingham. I don't dance very often," he admitted.

"You did very well, milord," she smiled encouragement.

"Would you like some lemonade?"

"Yes, thank you," she replied. Now, where was Sayward? Then she saw him dancing with the pretty brunette he had been friendly with at the last ball. Fenwick wandered away and Cassandra appeared at her side.

"Do you know who that brunette is?" Ruby asked. "I mean the one dancing with the tall man with a tanned complexion."

"Yes. That's Lady Arlington's daughter, Eleanor, very wealthy, and niece to a duke."

"Oh." Ruby's heart dropped. Why would Crispin even look at her with someone like that around?

Much to Ruby's surprise, when it came time for the midnight supper, she was delighted to find Crispin requesting the pleasure of her company. She took his arm and floated into the dining room trying to keep a demure smile on her face although she wanted to grin from ear to ear.

"I must compliment you on your dancing. I've noticed that you seem more confident with the steps than before."

"Thank you, milord. I am enjoying it this evening," Ruby said as she stole a look at Crispin's elegant profile. He was the picture of a perfect English gentleman. But what could she talk about? She felt so tongue-tied. There was a pause that went on too long. Then she remembered his recent expedition. "Did you bring back some interesting plants from the tropics, milord?"

"Yes. We did. A vast number of unusual plants grow there but I doubt many of them would survive in our cooler English climate. I will be trying to culture another species of orchid in my conservatory," he said.

"Is your glasshouse finished now, milord?"

"Yes, but I plan to add some slanted windows which will open for ventilation, now that I'm here to supervise the installation."

"Are you considering another trip back to Haiti in the future?"

"I would like to, very much, but I have obligations here at home which may prevent that happening. Also my mother has not been well," he replied.

Oh yes, the dragon she had heard about. Ruby glanced around the dining room and noticed an older lady holding a lorgnette up to her eyes and looking in her direction. Was that haughty woman his mother? Then, much to her dismay, she noticed that Crispin was staring towards the fireplace where Eleanor flirted with an older, portly gentleman. So that's why Crispin had asked her to accompany him in to supper, Eleanor already had an escort.

Ruby looked around the elegant dining room, far more opulent than at Thorncroft Hall. The dark panelled walls, lined with gilt framed paintings of hunting scenes, made the perfect foil for the long white linen covered table gleaming with silver. The dishes and cutlery reflected light from the tall beeswax candles in ornate polished candelabra. Soft violin music drifted in from the ballroom.

"Would you care for some ham? It's excellent?" Crispin said, holding up a platter.

Ruby had been so busy looking around the luxurious dining room that she hadn't focused on the food itself. She had expected a light meal but this was a veritable banquet. The only difference between this array of food and the dinner she had attended recently was that this was a cold repast. There were sliced hams, roast chicken, partridge, potted meats, savoury pies, jellied aspics and several Italian salads as well.

She nibbled at a little ham. It was delicious. But she didn't want Mme. Faure to have to let out the darts she had just put into her waistband. It would be so embarrassing.

Then the dessert course arrived, sweet wines for dunking the pasties accompanied it. Ruby restricted herself to one pistachio biscuit and a Prince of Wales wafer with its three-feather crest. She was disappointed. It looked better than it tasted. Then came the sorbets and ices, which Ruby forced herself to decline.

Crispin looked at her empty plate with concern. "I assure you the food here is of excellent quality."

"Yes, milord, I'm just not very hungry. I don't usually eat at this hour."

"Of course. Country hours versus city hours, but you'll get used to it. The trick is not to get up too early in the morning. In the city I rarely rise before noon."

A sudden vision of Crispin's head, hair tousled from sleep and a nightshirt open to reveal his bare chest, flashed through Ruby's mind. The fanciful thought brought a blush to her cheeks and she was filled with sudden longing for his touch. If she shared his bed she wouldn't want to get up till noon either. What a wicked idea but he looked good enough to eat.

During the carriage ride home at four in the morning Ruby was glad her aunt was fast asleep. She didn't want to talk about Crispin or Berrington. But the very next day two bouquets arrived and her aunt was there to comment.

"Pink carnations mean 'I will never forget you'. Who is that one from?"

"Sweets to the sweet, from Berrington," Ruby read aloud, handing her aunt the note.

"And the pansies?" her aunt asked.

"They're from Sayward and he writes, 'To a lovely young lady'."

"They mean 'think of me'. How very correct Lord Sayward is. But don't get your hopes up too high, Ruby. I noticed his mother eyeing you when you accompanied him in to supper. I'm sure she's making inquiries as we speak."

"How would she know my history?" Ruby asked.

"Your father is a member of the landed gentry, a country gentleman, but he is not a member of the aristocracy. She only has to look in Debrett's Peerage to verify that."

Chapter Five

⚮

Peter, Lord Berrington, sat in the bow window of Boodles, the London men's club to which he had just been admitted. He gazed around the oak panelled room filled with leather chairs and card tables. A coal fire burned in the hearth and its smell mingled with the aroma of expensive cigars. This was a male enclave for aristocrats seeking to forget, for a few hours, the pressures of domesticity, their mistresses and creditors. Several card games were in progress and making wagers was a popular pastime. The sums of money lost were enormous; Lord Whistbane had lost his townhouse only last week. The most interesting wagers involved women and horses. The Italian opera singer, Lady Arabella, was about to take a new lover. Currently the bets were on Lord Duren. His corset creaked when he arose from his chair but he had the most blunt to spend on her.

 Berrington sipped his brandy and pretended to read The Morning Post as bits of gossip drifted around him. He could thank his sister's godparents for sponsoring his membership here and also fate, which had decreed that he was next in line to inherit both Linden Hall and the title that came with it. The English were a curious lot. They didn't welcome newcomers with open arms and the fact that he spoke with an Irish accent seemed to make matters worse.

His ears perked up when he heard the name 'Sayward'. Wasn't that the lord who had danced with pretty Ruby Gillingham last week? He had seemed quite taken with her. Berrington moved closer, sitting next to the fire, the better to hear the conversation.

"Heard it from Sayward himself that he's setting up a love nest in Russell Square. Said she'd be his by Michaelmas. Ellington bet him twenty pounds to the contrary and Sayward took the bet." The man chuckled.

"Who is she?" the other voice asked.

"Some young thing fresh from the country, Thorncroft Hall I think he said."

Berrington almost choked on his brandy. They were talking about Ruby Gillingham.

***

Ruby could hardly contain her excitement. She had received an invitation to a ball to be held tonight at Crispin's London town house, which according to Aunt Ada, was very grand. The prospect was exhilarating but frightening. She picked at her food. If her aunt noticed her loss of appetite she made no comment. But later when dressing, her maid confirmed that Ruby's waistline was diminishing.

"Lace me up, as tight as you can, Abby," Ruby said. "I must look my very best." She wore her first silk gown in the palest shade of periwinkle blue.

***

When they arrived at the Sayward's, Ruby was first received by Crispin.

"You must save me a dance," he whispered as his eyes caressed hers over the hand he had just brought to his lips.

"I'll be happy to, my lord," Ruby replied.

Next in line was Lady Sayward, Crispin's mother. Ruby curtseyed demurely but received a frosty welcome. Was it because Crispin had just kissed her hand? Aunt Ada was oblivious as she was caught up in the throng of greeting other attendees. No help there, so Ruby made herself as inconspicuous as possible and followed in the wake of her aunt as she sallied forth into the ornate reception rooms.

Halfway through the evening Crispin appeared at Ruby's side to claim his dance, a quadrille. The music stopped all too soon, but much to Ruby's surprised delight, as he escorted her to the side of the ballroom he whispered, "I wish to speak to you in private. Can you meet me in the green study in about ten minutes?"

Ruby nodded, speechless, then had the presence of mind to ask, "Where is it, milord? This is my first time in your home."

"Of course, I had forgotten that. Go to the front balcony but instead of stepping outside take the hallway which leads to the right, then take the second door to your right again." He bowed and turned away from her.

Bubbling with excitement Ruby mingled with the crush of people. What could Crispin have in mind? Perhaps he meant to propose? This did seem a little improper. He hadn't even asked permission to court her. She knew that was normally first step but Ruby wasn't going to dwell on it. Wild horses wouldn't stop her from keeping this rendezvous. Ten minutes he had said. She just had time to go to the ladies' retiring room and make sure every curl was in place. Maybe she could tug her décolletage down a little?

Ruby had the room to herself and quickly adjusted her bodice as best she could. Her hair looked fine and her cheeks were a becoming shade of pink from dancing. She tucked a wisp of hair into her chignon and turned to see Lettice, the elder of the Sarne sisters, entering the room. She averted her eyes but not soon enough.

"My, you are getting fashionable," Lettice said. "It won't do you any good, though. Lady Sayward has been making inquiries about you and I was happy to enlighten her."

"Whatever do you mean?" Ruby asked as a tight knot began to form in her stomach.

"Oh, I think you know. You're a commoner, that's all."

"My father is Sir Roderick – ," Ruby began before being cut off.

"- But your mother wasn't a lady, was she?" Lettice said with venom in her voice.

"Why are you like this? What have I ever done to you?" Ruby asked.

"Like what?" Lettice gave her an innocent look as she patted her already tidy hair. "I'm simply telling the truth – and you know it."

Ruby felt her cheeks flush as her temper rose. She opened her mouth to use the most colourful swear word her father's stable boys used. Then stopped. She clamped her mouth closed and ran from the room instead.

Oh dear! The ten minutes had likely elapsed. Would Crispin be waiting still? Now, where had she been told to go? To the front balcony, then right, or was it left? No. Surely, it was two rights? Wasn't it?

She let herself into the study with relief and as she looked around she realized how it got its name. Virtually everything was green from the walls, to the curtains, to the carpet. Only the polished mahogany desk and leather chair were not. She started pacing in front of the fireplace. Was she too late? Had he already come and gone? Then the door opened softly and he was there, Crispin, Lord Sayward, the breathtakingly handsome aristocrat.

He walked slowly toward her, his even pace mesmerizing. His be-witching grey eyes swept over her from head to toe. As he came close she could smell his cologne and some very expensive tobacco. Her heart was beating so fast she could barely breathe. He took her hand and kissed it through her evening glove.

"Oh no, that's not good enough. Do you mind?" Looking into her eyes, he peeled it off slowly and kissed her hand again, first on the back and then on her palm. She could feel his lips and breath on her skin. She shivered with delight.

"For days now I've wanted to tell you how I feel but when we meet it's never private enough." His voice was low and gravelly sending shivers up her spine.

"I know," Ruby whispered.

"I find you the most enchanting young lady of my acquaintance. I long to spend time with you, to have intimate moments alone. Do you understand what I am asking of you?" He gazed ever deeper into her eyes.

If this was a marriage proposal, something wasn't right. "I think so, but shouldn't you speak to my Aunt Ada or my father first?"

"Oh you misunderstand my meaning, I ache for us to spend blissful afternoons together, Ruby. I've already rented a charming townhouse in Russell Square. I shall send you notes telling you when to meet me there and you will tell your aunt that you are having tea at Gunter's with a girlfriend. How does that sound?"

Ruby's romantic dreams came crashing to the ground. "Are you asking me to be your mistress? I thought you were about to propose marriage." Her tears began bubbling up and her throat constricted so much that she could hardly breathe.

"Oh lovely Ruby, you must know that marriage between us is out of the question."

"Why?" Ruby glared at him.

He seemed taken aback, as if he hadn't expected this from her but she had to hear him put it into words.

"Ruby, dearest, I have a duty, as head of my family, to bring prestige to our lineage. I thought you understood. I'm sorry but I must marry someone who is at least my social equal." At least he had the grace to look uncomfortable.

"And I'm not?" Ruby bit off. "But neither will I stoop to become anyone's mistress. I thought you loved me." She fought back a sob and just managed to choke out, "I never want to set eyes on you again."

She burst into tears and ran from the room sobbing. Turning a corner in the hallway she stopped to catch her breath. No one must see her like this. Whatever would people think? Questions would be asked. She caught the sleeve of a passing butler.

"Please tell Lady Paxton that her niece has been taken ill, she's one of the chaperones sitting along the far wall. Have her meet me at the edge of the front balcony. Right away! Please hurry!"

Ruby wiped away her tears with the little scrap of lacy handkerchief in her reticule and then realized that she was still clutching her glove, the one that Crispin had removed. Quickly she pulled it on and, taking a deep breath, she crept out into the cool evening air on the balcony, hoping no one would see her.

A long time passed and still her aunt hadn't come. Her breathing slowly returned to normal and she decided that perhaps she could go back inside. But what a strange society this was. A born gentleman could treat you as a plaything rather than a person just because your lineage didn't measure up to his. It made her wonder whom could she trust. She turned around and there was Berrington coming towards her.

"Where have you been, Miss Gillingham? I know that I arrived late but I was hoping you would have room on your dance card for me." He smiled at her in his flattering way.

"I'm sorry but I feel rather ill. I'm waiting for my aunt to take me home." Ruby said hoping she didn't look as miserable as she felt.

"Stay right there. I shall find your aunt." He hurried off and returned in moments, her aunt following at an almost un-ladylike pace.

"Ruby, whatever is the matter? You look so flushed," her aunt said.

"I'm not well, aunt. Please, I need to go home, right away."

"Of course, my dear. The carriage may take some time to meet us at the door but we can wait in the front vestibule."

"I will order your carriage," Berrington said as he bowed and hastily disappeared back into the crush of people.

"Could it be something you ate, child?" her aunt asked, looking worried.

"No, no, aunt. I'll explain in the carriage. I just need to

leave here immediately." They made their way slowly to the front hallway where Berrington was already waiting.

"The carriage is on its way to you. I'll keep an eye out for it." He stepped outside the main doorway. The delay was excruciating for Ruby but at last Berrington returned with news of its arrival. He helped them into the carriage and saw them off.

***

Berrington felt responsible. He was almost sure that Sayward had just propositioned Ruby Gillingham at the ball. Could he have prevented it, somehow? He had struggled with the information he had overheard recently at Boodles but how could he have warned her without causing more distress? He couldn't just go up to her and say, "Sayward is going to ask you to be his mistress." And why would she believe him, after all they were simply neighbours. Also, he had hoped that something would prevent it happening. Now he wasn't so sure. He would give a lot to know what had actually happened between Sayward and Miss Gillingham. He would send her flowers in the hopes that she would be able to put this ugliness behind When Peter finally got to the Dabbley's town home the butler informed him that his Lordship was in the library and wished to speak with him. What could that be about? He must thank him again for sponsoring his membership to Boodles. It was an amazing source of information. He made his way to the library.

"Ah, Berrington, come in," Lord Dabbley said heartily. "Will you have a drink with me?"

"Yes. Thank you, milord," Berrington said. Lord Dabbley had an excellent cellar. After they had raised their glasses in a toast together, Lord Dabbley said, "I have some news that I'm afraid you will find disturbing."

"Oh, really?" Berrington asked.

"I'm sorry to be the bearer of such bad news but a challenge has been issued regarding the validity of your claim to be Lord Berrington and owner of the entailed property, Linden Hall."

"But I didn't lay claim to the title," Berrington clarified. "I was notified that I was the next in line."

"Nevertheless we need to confirm the path to your inheritance. I understand that it's from your mother's side of the family?"

"Yes. It is. My Mother was one of five daughters."

"A challenge of this type usually focuses on the legality of the marriage. Were your patents married in England and can you get written proof?"

"My parents eloped to Ireland, with my aunt as chaperone and were married in an Anglican church in Dublin once they arrived. I may be able to get proof but I would need to go to Ireland. I believe my aunt still has some of my mother's things."

"Then I think you had better get yourself on the next boat, young man. This must be attended to post haste."

"I will milord, of course, but may I ask who is challenging my claim?"

"Yes, of course. It's Lord Sayward."

Berrington swore out loud.

"I see you are acquainted with the man," Lord Dabbley said as he raised his eyebrows.

"Not personally, no, however I have encountered him socially and have heard gossip." He wasn't going to divulge what he suspected about Sayward. He was a greedy bastard. Didn't he already have enough land and estates to his name?

***

In the carriage Ruby started to sob and couldn't seem to stop the tears. "Oh aunt. I was so shocked and…"

"There, there child. It can't be that bad. Tell me what happened."

Gulping back tears, Ruby nodded. "He asked me to be his mistress!" She choked out the words and started crying again.

"Who? Berrington?" her aunt asked.

'No. Crispin! Lord Sayward," she added. "I thought he'd arranged for us to meet privately to propose marriage – not to proposition me."

"My dear Ruby, marriage proposals don't happen in secret rendezvous and require the consent of your parent or guardian."

"I know that but I've been I love with him for so long and I thought he loved me too." Ruby paused to blow her nose hard and take a deep breath to focus her thoughts. "But I made him explain why he couldn't marry me. He said he had a duty to his family to marry someone who was at least his social equal. Obviously I don't qualify. Everything was arranged. He had rented a townhouse where we could spend afternoons alone together." She started crying again.

"Now, now, dear. Did anyone see you going to meet him?"

"No. I was careful. We met in the green study and left separately."

"Good. Then there will not be any gossip to deal with," her aunt said with obvious relief.

"I hate this! Having to be careful what others think. I want to shout from the rooftops that Sayward dared to proposition me," Ruby said in a stubborn voice.

"No, no, dear. That's the last thing you should do. The only way forward is to pretend it never happened."

"I'm going to give him the cut direct next time I see him." Ruby declared.

"Ruby, Ruby. Even that's not a good idea. People will wonder why."

"I don't care, aunt. He hurt my feelings and I'd like to get even. He's probably going to marry Eleanor, the duke's niece and have a string of mistresses."

"There's nothing you can do about that, Ruby dear, and you shouldn't even try."

When they got to Crescent Street Ruby went straight to her room. She couldn't sleep so she decided to write a long letter to Penelope. It took both sides of two sheets of paper. At least she could tell her everything.

The next day Aunt Ada announced that they were to call on Lady Dainsbury and her granddaughter. But Ruby begged to be excused knowing she wouldn't be good company. Cassandra would want to discuss last night's ball in minute detail and she was afraid she'd blurt out the whole incident with Crispin, which her aunt had strictly forbidden her to mention.

Chapter Six

After her aunt left, Ruby sat in her room feeling wretched. She had written to Penelope last night but still felt miserable. What else could she do to make this dreadful turmoil in her heart go away? She kept thinking about the scene in the green study, kept repeating Crispin's unkind words. If she were home at Thorncroft Hall she would go down to the kitchen and lose herself in baking a lovely cake or making scones. Perhaps she could do that here? Her aunt was out for at least two hours and the servants seemed to like her well enough. Perhaps, like at home, they would keep her baking a secret? She crept downstairs.

Becky, the scullery maid, confirmed that cook had gone to the market for fresh fish. Excellent! Ruby asked Becky to show her where cook kept the sugar, butter and eggs, also to bring her a mixing bowl, a wooden spoon and some cake pans. Soon she was happily creaming the sugar and butter together. Already she could feel her spirits rising. She checked the stove and had the maid add more coal to make it hotter. She separated the eggs and beat the whites until they were stiff. As she folded the flour into the whites and added the egg mixture she sang happily to herself. She scraped the batter into the pans and was just putting them into the oven when she heard a cry behind her.

"What's this? What a terrible mess! I have dinner to prepare and tea to lay out. And who's that under the mob cap and wearing my apron?"

Ruby pulled off the borrowed cap and faced the cook's wrath. "I'm sorry Mrs. Bolton. But at home I am allowed to bake if the kitchen is not in use. I know I should have asked your permission but you were out. I have just put a sponge cake in the oven. It should be baked at half past five."

"Well, I never. A young lady who knows how to bake a cake? Her ladyship didn't tell me that you would take over my kitchen and I don't think she'll like it either. You mark my words, Miss."

"Couldn't you keep this a secret between us, Mrs. Bolton?" Ruby begged.

"No. I could not. I'm that loyal to her ladyship. She's a good mistress. Now out you go, young lady. You don't belong here, below stairs."

Crestfallen, Ruby turned to go. Then she looked back at the scowling cook. "The cake would be good with jam between the layers and just a dusting of sugar on top."

Mrs. Bolton sniffed and turned her back. As Ruby went sadly back upstairs she heard the cook shouting at Becky to wash the table off at once.

When Aunt Ada came home Ruby stayed in her room. Soon a maid came to tell her that her ladyship wished to speak with her in the drawing room immediately. Her aunt was pacing up and down in front of the fireplace.

"Whatever has come over you, Ruby, upsetting Mrs. Bolton like that? I've never seen her in such a state."

"I'm sorry aunt, but I was so unhappy and baking always makes me feel better."

"I've never heard of such a thing. It's not what ladies do. It's servants' work. I value Mrs. Bolton but she's not my equal. Why would you lower yourself to her level? You've really made her angry by invading her part of the house. I never go down to the kitchens. She comes up to the breakfast room when it's time to discuss menus with me."

"But I love to bake. The happiest memories I have of my Mother are of baking with her when I was young." Ruby's eyes flooded with tears and she looked down to hide them.

"Oh child, this will not do. Perhaps you could get away with it out in the country but this is London and servants talk. It's just not ladylike."

"I'm sorry, Aunt Ada. I won't do it again. I promise." Ruby said.

"See that you don't and we'll say no more about it. Now let's have some tea." her aunt said ringing the bell.

Jarvis carried in the tea tray a few minutes later and there was Ruby's cake dusted with icing sugar, sitting beside the tea pot. It looked beautiful. Ruby's eyes widened and she waited. Her aunt ate a mouthful but remained silent. Ruby sampled the cake herself. It was good. She couldn't help herself and blurted out "Do you like the cake, aunt?"

"Yes. It's fine. Mrs. Bolton always makes good teatime sweets. Why do you ask?"

"This is my cake. I baked this." Ruby announced proudly. "See? It's still warm from the oven. I put it into the oven just as Mrs. Bolton came home from the market. She hasn't had time to make it since she came home."

"Child what am I to do with you? Ladies don't bake cakes."

"But couldn't you at least tell me that it's a good cake?" Ruby bit her lip and waited for her aunt to say something. Her aunt heaved a sigh and took another bite of cake.

"Delicious it may be, but as I said earlier, ladies do not bake cakes."

***

The next day, flowers arrived with a note. Ruby was so sure they were from Crispin that she almost threw them in the waste basket but stopped at the last moment. To her surprise they were from Berrington, not Crispin. The note read, "Bouquets of good health and happiness, Berrington." Her aunt came bustling in at that moment and saw the bouquet of deep purple and creamy white blossoms.

"Yarrow and heliotrope. How unusual. Yarrow means 'cure for a broken heart' and heliotrope stands for 'devoted affection'. I think that Berrington has a tendre for you, my dear."

"The whole marriage mart sickens me, aunt," Ruby said. "I enjoyed dancing with Berrington but I just can't think about him or any man, right now. Maybe I should go home."

"Oh no, dear. The Little Season is not even half way through. It goes until early November when fox hunting season begins. You'll feel better in a day or two. Why don't we get you a new dress? Your figure has slimmed down so nicely."

When they arrived at her shop, Aunt Ada's modiste was, of course, delighted to see them.

"Some new fabrics have just arrived for the fall season. This copper colour will be flattering with your chestnut hair, don't you think?" Mme. Faure held up a length of moiré taffeta in a rust and royal blue pattern.

"Yes. It's very pretty but I don't need another frock right now," Ruby said rather despondently. She didn't feel like dressing up or attending social events.

"Nonsense, child. Every girl can use a new dress. We are expected for dinner on Sunday at Lord and Lady Upton's and there will fireworks on the terrace after sunset. You will enjoy it." Clearly, her aunt really wanted to go, so she made no further objections.

***

On the morning of the Upton's dinner party, Ruby woke early, still desperately unhappy. Every night for the past week she had dreamt of Sayward. She was at a ball when his betrothal to Eleanor, Lady Arlington's daughter, was announced or she was in a crowd watching Sayward and his new bride getting into his carriage after their wedding. Once she had even dreamt she was in the church and had tried to stop their marriage ceremony. Would this never end? She gave a little sob and dried her eyes. This was why she didn't want to attend any more social events. She would see Sayward for sure and she couldn't bear the thought. However, she was obligated and must do as her aunt wished for Aunt Ada had been so good to her.

Ruby's new rust taffeta rustled as she walked unenthusiastically down the stairs at Crescent Street. Yes. It was pretty and brought out the auburn highlights in her hair but she took little delight in wearing it. When they got to the Upton's opulent villa, on the outskirts of the city, Ruby was impressed but had no desire ever to be the mistress of such a grand house. Immediately her aunt struck up a conversation with Lady Dainsbury but Cassandra was not beside her grandmother. Ruby scanned the rapidly filling ballroom but she was nowhere to be seen. But then, she felt a tap on her shoulder. It was

Caitlin. What luck! Just the person she had been hoping to see.

"I haven't seen you at the last few events. Have you been ill?" Caitlin asked with a note of genuine concern.

"Yes, in a manner of speaking," Ruby admitted. In front of this crowd she couldn't very well say she was sick of the ton, sick of the marriage mart. "It's just that I'd like to go home, back to Kent. What about you?"

"Oh, I knew from the start that a Season in London wasn't for me but Lady Sally insisted and even my brother, Peter, agreed it was a good idea."

Berrington. Would he be here? "Is your brother still in town?"

"No. He left today for Dublin."

"Left for Ireland? Whatever for?" Ruby asked.

"It's something to do with the title he inherited. I didn't quite understand it myself."

A jolt of disappointment surprised Ruby. She hadn't realized, let alone admitted to herself, how much she had been looking forward to seeing Berrington again. Perhaps because he wasn't part of the ton when she met him she found him more sincere and trustworthy?

"When will he be back?" she asked.

"I don't know, but I have a problem myself. It's Lord Dulsin. Things are more serious than I thought. He has been flirting with me for a while now but I didn't realize he'd asked my godfather's permission to court me, officially. Now he's proposed marriage and both Lady Sally and her husband advise me to accept, saying it's a good offer."

"And do you want to?"

"I can't, Ruby. It's one thing to flirt at a dance but it's

entirely another to share a bed and breakfast with a man for the rest of my life."

"Is he repulsive?" Ruby asked.

"No. But it's just not right. I can't really explain, but I don't even like to hold hands with him."

"Then you should definitely say no."

"But Lady Sally says he has a lovely townhouse and I could continue taking harp lessons from the best teachers when we're in London."

"Those aren't good enough reasons."

"I know but what can I do? Peter's away and Lord Dulsin expects an answer. Oh dear. Here he comes."

Ruby watched as an older man with a receding hairline approached them. His eyes were focused on Caitlin with an intensity that reminded Ruby of a hungry starling about to pounce on an unsuspecting bug.

"Miss Trigan, good evening. How lovely to see you again," he said bowing deeply.

"Good evening Lord Dulsin," Caitlin replied curtseying. "May I introduce my good friend Miss Gillingham? She's from Kent."

Dulsin's hooded gaze rested on her bosom a few seconds too long even before greeting her. "Good evening Miss Gillingham. Charmed, I'm sure," he said giving her a slow predatory smile. Ruby bobbed a curtsey already feeling uncomfortable. Luckily she was saved from further conversation because just then the butler announced that dinner was served. Lord Dulsin took his eyes off Ruby, then offered his arm to Caitlin. Poor thing, what could she do but accept?

"Miss Gillingham?" a male voice asked from behind. "May I have the pleasure of taking you in to dinner?"

Ruby turned to look into the hesitant but rather kindly

face of Lord Fenwick. "Why thank you, milord," she replied with relief, as she accompanied him into the dining room.

When they found a place at the table, Ruby noticed that Lettice Sarne was very pleased with herself; she looked like a cat toying with a canary because she was sitting with Lord Trafferton. At least there would be no call to converse for they were seated down the table from them. Then she saw Sayward. Her heart sank. He was wiling his charms on a very pretty, young girl who had just arrived from Sussex and the girl seemed totally dazzled by his attention. Ruby knew that he was trolling for a mistress and his actions made her nauseous. Suddenly, she felt stifled by the crowded drawing room and feared she would be physically sick. That would be so embarrassing. Determined not to even glance in Sayward's direction again Ruby turned her attention back to Lord Fenwick. "Is your garden prepared for the winter, milord?" she asked, glad they at least had one common interest.

The dinner was excellent but Ruby neither knew what she ate nor barely tasted it. She carried on a very predictable conversation with Fenwick and agreed with the stolid gentleman to the left as he rattled on about his bloodhounds. Was Caitlin faring any better with Lord Dulsin? Would this interminable dinner ever end? Only half listening to the conversation around her, Ruby began formulating a getaway plan.

When everyone gathered on the Upton's terrace for the fireworks display Ruby manoeuvred her way to stand close to Caitlin. "We need to talk," she whispered. "I have a plan that will help us both escape from this. Can you meet me in Hyde Park tomorrow? Take your maid and just tell Lady

Sally that you need a breath of fresh air. If not tomorrow, then the next but I'd rather it was tomorrow."

"Yes. I think I could." Caitlin looked dubious. "I'll send you a note to confirm but I must go." She glanced over Ruby's shoulder, gave a small shudder, ducked down then began to move away through the dinner guests as Lord Dulsin bore down on them.

Ruby's mind was in a turmoil but of one thing she was certain. Both she and Caitlin needed to get out of London – as soon as possible. Her aunt had arranged her meeting with Fenwick tonight, just as surely as Caitlin's godparents were promoting Lord Dulsin's suit.

***

The next day when they met in the park, Caitlin ran into Ruby's arms and burst into tears. Ruby hugged her close then turned to their maids. "Can you walk about thirty paces behind us, please? I'll make it worth your while."

The maids nodded and fell back while Caitlin and Ruby walked on ahead, arm in arm. When they got to a park bench they stopped and sat down. Looking back, they saw their maids chatting with a group of nursery maids wheeling baby carriages. Good; they were occupied.

"Whatever's happened, Caitlin?" Ruby asked.

"I'm desperate. Dulsin won't take no for an answer. I think he's in a business venture of some sort with Lord Dabbley, and now my godparents are on his side. Lady Sally says I don't have a good reason for refusing him. And the latest thing is he wants to change my name to Catherine, a good English name. I like my name just the way it is, thank you."

"So do I, Caitlin. So do I." Ruby nodded. "I understand what you're saying and I sympathize. My aunt really favours Lord Fenwick's suit. It was no accident that he was my dinner partner last night. But I have a solution. Let's run away together – back to Thorncroft Hall, my home in Kent. Father will be disappointed at first, as he hoped I'd find a husband but he'll be happy to see me all the same. I know he will."

"But what about me?" Caitlin asked. "I can't stay with you forever."

"Why ever not?" Ruby teased, then added. "But you won't have to. Your brother's estate, Linden Hall is only twenty minutes away from Thorncroft by horse and buggy. We shall be neighbours. As soon as Berrington returns from Ireland you can go and live with him."

Caitlin looked more hopeful. "But there's some problem with his claim to the title, what if –"

"—We'll deal with that later," Ruby said firmly. "Right now we need to leave London and here's how we shall do it." She leaned over and whispered. When she's finished, Caitlin hugged Ruby again, this time in relief.

"You are amazing, Ruby. Do you think it will work?"

"I don't see why not. All we need is money for the coach. Do you have any?"

"A little. I'm given pin money."

"So am I and this week's will go to bribe our maids. But I'll pawn my mother's pearl earrings if necessary."

***

Ruby mulled over the question of disguises. Caitlin's red hair must be hidden; it stood out like a flag. Perhaps a hat with a heavy veil like mourners wore? But where would she find something like that? Wait. Aunt Ada was a widow. Maybe she still had her widow's weeds.

When she got back to Crescent Street, her aunt was out visiting so Ruby decided to look in the attic. It seemed a likely place to start her search. Pleased to see a bit of light coming from the small round window under the eaves, she looked around at the dusty cobweb covered boxes and trunks. Yes. The trunks might hold old clothes.

The first one was brass-bound and looked as if it had weathered many a long journey. When the clasp finally yielded to her efforts Ruby was disappointed. It contained journals, letters and books of a seafaring nature. When she opened the next trunk she caught her breath. The top layer had several beautiful ball gowns made of satin, lace and tulle. These must have been from Aunt Ada's days as a debutante. What fun it would be to wear these old pannier style dresses to a costume ball. Ruby lifted them out carefully and set them to one side as she continued to look through the layers of petticoats and chemises. Right at the bottom of the trunk, almost hidden, she found what she had been searching for.

Ruby gently lifted out Aunt Ada's black dresses, hats, veils, lace mittens, black fans and even a reticule decorated with black jet beads. She put one complete outfit aside, right down to the black trimmed petticoat. Caitlin was about the same height as Aunt Ada, though a lot slimmer, perhaps a pillow or a rolled up blanket would suffice? She found a black shawl and made a bundle of all the clothing. If she added a black veil to the dress she had worn when she arrived from Kent, she would appear to be in half mourning, which would protect her identity as well. Bless Aunt Ada for having more than one mourning costume. She took another veiled hat and shawl from the trunk, then carefully replaced everything else. Wrapping their disguises in the shawl, she carefully hid the bundle out of sight but within easy reach near the attic door.

Next, Ruby considered the question of how to pay for

their escape. Ruefully she realized that their pin money, even when combined, would not be enough. She would need to pawn her mother's pearl ear bobs, after all. She hated the idea but could think of no alternative. How to find and get to a pawnshop? She would need to enlist help.

"Abby, I need your assistance," she said when her maid came to dress her for dinner. "But you must promise to keep this a secret. No one in this house must know."

"I promise, miss. Is it a young man?" her maid's eyes sparkled with mischief.

"No, not exactly. Actually I'm trying to avoid a certain gentleman."

Her maid's face fell but she then eyed Ruby curiously.

"I need you to take me to a pawnshop."

"Yes, miss. I can do that but it's in a pretty rough part of town. Are you sure?"

"That doesn't matter. When can we go?" Ruby asked.

"My next half day off is tomorrow afternoon. We could go then."

"Perfect," Ruby smiled. "But remember. Not a word to anyone. Just come and tell me when you're ready tomorrow. I'll make sure I'm free."

***

The next morning when Ruby came down for breakfast, flowers had arrived for her again, this time a lovely bouquet of Michaelmas daisies. She smiled at their rich purple hue, which reminded her of the gardens at Thorncroft Hall. Aunt Ada came bustling in.

"Michaelmas daisies signify farewell. Who could be sending you these, Ruby? Surely not Lord Fenwick."

"No, Aunt. It's not Lord Fenwick." She handed her aunt the accompanying card. It read,

"Dear Miss Gillingham,
I must go away for a short time but look forward to seeing you on my return to London.
Your faithful servant,
Berrington"

"I wondered what had become of him," her aunt said.

Ruby didn't think her aunt would care about Berrington's inheritance issues but she hoped things would be resolved quickly as she would dearly like to see Linden Hall and the estate restored to its former glory.

***

The next day Ruby informed her aunt that she was going take advantage of the break in the weather and take another walk with her maid. She and Abby made their way through streets that became seedier, narrower and more crowded with beggars as they continued.

Finally, Abby pointed towards a rather dark and very dingy little shop. A sign with three brass balls hung above the grubby doorway. They had arrived. A bell rang as they opened the door and a burly man with mustachios appeared behind the counter. The pawnbroker grunted when they entered. "Eh? What have ye got fur me?" he said.

Ruby reluctantly took out her mother's earrings and placed them on the table with trembling fingers. She winced when the proprietor's large dirty hands closed on them.

"Aye. They'll sell," he wheezed.

He reached into his coin box and extracted two coins and dropped them on the table.

"That's all ye get."

Ruby grabbed the money and muttered to Abby, "Come. We must go."

As they made a hurried exit, Ruby hoped that this would be enough money for two fares on the stagecoach. "Are we anywhere near Lad's Lane?" she asked Abby.

"Yes. It's really close by, only two streets away. Why?"

"I must get to an inn called the 'Swan with the Two Heads'. I have to purchase some stagecoach tickets." Her maid looked as if she were about to ask further questions but Ruby cut her off with, "It's best you don't know."

"This way, then," Abby replied.

They arrived at the inn and Abby showed Ruby where to book the tickets. Ruby was surprised to find that each ticket holder had to be named. On the spur of the moment she decided that she and Caitlin would be the Lady and Miss Serena Fenton, an older woman in deep mourning travelling with her niece. After paying a deposit of half the cost for each ticket, Ruby was relieved to find that there would be more than enough money for the rest of the fare.

Chapter Seven

Berrington watched as the skyline of Dublin appeared through the mist. His ship, the Merriweather, was due to dock by noon. He could see the outline of a gothic cathedral with its characteristic flying buttresses stretching out like wings on either side. That must be Christ Church Cathedral, which was located slightly upstream from the port which was on the left bank of the River Liffey. His parents had been married in Dublin, perhaps right there in Christ Church. Lord Dabbley had impressed upon him the need to resolve his inheritance issue with all due haste so it would be prudent to begin his enquiries there. If the cathedral had any record of their nuptials it might save him a lot of time. And to say he didn't trust Sayward was an understatement.

He had meant to write his Aunt Margaret, in Glendalough, to tell her of his arrival but things being as they were, he knew that he would arrive in Ireland about the same time as the post. He would surprise her instead, time permitting. But if the cathedral could answer his question, there would be no need to find his aunt at all.

On the other hand if he could provide physical proof, preferably the marriage license or certificate, would that help to solidify his claim? Peter's aunt had approved of her sister's elopement and made her parents' marriage less scandalous by being their chaperone. Might his aunt have kept either the licence or certificate amongst his mother's things?

His thoughts drifted to Ruby. He hoped that she had recovered from Sayward's selfish proposition. He wished that this trip to Ireland hadn't come up just now. He had sent flowers but wished he could be there for her.

The docks were getting closer now so he went down to his cabin to collect this things. He had travelled light. Eager to begin, Berrington picked up his travel bag, nimbly navigated the steep gangplank between ship and dock, then strode up the street looking for an inn for the night. The Green Dragon looked inviting. Perhaps they would know when the next stage left for Glendalough? The innkeeper confirmed that a stage left at six in the morning. But he was getting ahead of himself; first things first, a visit to the cathedral to check the registers.

As he approached the impressive building he saw a man in black robes leaving a side door. Berrington caught up to him.

"Excuse me, Reverend, but I wonder if you might help?" he asked bowing.

"Perhaps, my son. What do you seek?" the priest answered.

"My parents were married in Dublin twenty-eight years ago. I'm not sure which church but I do know that my aunt was one of their witnesses. I need proof of their marriage."

The older man looked Berrington with new interest.

"You are not from here yet I detect a touch of Gaelic in your speech."

"Yes, I now live in the south of England, in Kent, but I grew up here. I arrived today by boat."

"Welcome back to Dublin, my son. I am Father Brennan, at your service. If your parents were wed in this cathedral a record of their marriage will be in our parish register. Follow me."

The priest led the way down a side aisle of the cathedral to an alcove near a door leading to the sacristy. An enormous leather bound book sat on a stand in the corner. Father Brennan slowly turned the pages back to the year 1790. "What were their names, now?"

"My father was Edward Trigan of the diocese of Glendalough. My mother's maiden name was Dorothy Josephine Sarton of Kent, England."

The priest carefully turned more pages. Then he looked again more closely. "Aha!" he exclaimed. "Here we are – the sixth of May 1790 with Reverend Tolmie officiating. You are in luck, young man."

Relief swept through Berrington. Thank God! Thank God! He could keep Linden Hall and the title. He could court Ruby in earnest. But then he stopped. "How can I prove this, father? Is there a certificate you can give me to take back to England?" he asked.

"No, my son. That is not within my power. The bishop himself will have to confirm this for you but at present he is attending a terminally ill friend's last hours and cannot be disturbed. You will have to wait." He looked at Berrington's crest fallen face and continued. "I may have more news later. Call on me this evening, I will be conducting evensong here at seven o'clock."

"Thank you, Father Brennan. I'll do that," Berrington

bowed and left the cathedral. He made his way back to the Green Dragon and, with a lighter heart, decided to have a pint.

He settled himself with a tankard of ale and looked around. He heard familiar laughter coming from the next table. Could that be Clooney? Sure enough, it was. He was one of the farm labourers on his cousin's land. Although neither Roger, his cousin, nor his uncle approved, Peter had befriended Clooney, who had a sharp wit and could see the ridiculous side of life.

"Clooney, how is it that you're here – instead of Glendalough?"

"Peter! 'Tis you is it, after all this time? I came with Lady Margaret who had some shopping to do. She needed someone to drive the dog cart."

"My Aunt Margaret is here? Now?"

"Aye. She's staying at the Gibson Hotel up the street."

"Thank you, Clooney. I'll see you later." Berrington downed the rest of his ale in one gulp and fairly ran up the street. He entered the Gibson Hotel and asked for Lady Trigan.

"Room seven at the top of the stairs," the innkeeper said.

Berrington knocked at the door to room seven. "Tell Lady Trigan that her nephew, Peter, is here."

Aunt Margaret dragged him into the room and hugged him. "Peter! How wonderful! What are you doing here? Come, sit down." She took his hand and led him to a settee in front of the hearth. "Susanna. Put some more coal on the fire," she said. "Now Peter, tell me all. I'm delighted to see you but I doubt that I'm the reason for your visit. I thought you would be busy at your new estate in Kent, Linden Hall, is it?"

"Yes, aunt. That's why I'm here. My right to inherit Linden Hall has been challenged and I need proof of my parents' marriage. Can you help me?"

"Let me think," his aunt said, her expression turning serious. "Your father purchased a marriage license and they were wed at Christ Church within three days of arriving here. I still have the license among your mother's things but that's all. Can the cathedral help?"

"That's just it, Aunt. They do have the marriage recorded in their parish registry but the bishop has to confirm it himself and he's not available at present – a dying friend."

"I see. And you need this as soon as can be? I go home tomorrow and could send it to you on the return stage, might that do?"

"Thank you, yes. The license will give additional proof and I fear I need everything I can get. This affects my whole life."

"I know, Peter. I was so very happy for you when I heard of the inheritance. You were the one with so little to establish yourself in the world since your father was a second son. Now, can you stay and have supper with me tonight?"

"Yes, aunt, after I call at the cathedral. Father Brennan may have some news just before evensong."

"Good, I need to go to the dry goods store in town with Susanna here but will order dinner for us both after you've spoken with him." She gave him a radiant smile and he kissed her hand before taking his departure.

Now that he had a few hours to fill he wanted to find Clooney. He had a lot of questions that needed answers. Why was Aunt Margaret here with only her maid? Why wasn't Roger, the new Lord Trigan with her, or his wife?

He remembered something about a betrothal before he left for Oxford but that was two years ago, perhaps he hadn't married yet? He walked back towards the Green Dragon Inn and spotted Clooney standing on the dock looking out to sea. He hailed him and they walked along the pier leading to the Poolbeg Lighthouse.

"What's it like, now, with Roger as your new master?" he asked Clooney.

"Bad, right bad. The old lord was strict but mostly fair. This toff makes us work longer hours so we have no time to work our own plots and hardly lets us keep any food for the winter. Some folks was almost starving before spring come this year. I might just run away to sea, anything to get away."

"I'm sorry to hear that. I'd hire you myself, Clooney, but I have to prove that I inherited Linden Hall fair and square. If I can't do that I'm back to being a penniless law student at Oxford."

"Even toffs like you have problems," Clooney said with a smile that grew wider at Peter's next words.

"How true. Look I'll be in touch with Lady Trigan. She can let you know if I've solved my problems. When I do, I'll send you the fare to come work on my estate."

Later that evening, Peter met his Aunt Margaret at the Gibson Hotel as arranged. She had reserved a private dining room and looked up happily when he walked in. "Come in, dear. I hope you have good news for me."

He shook his head. "No, not yet, aunt. The bishop is still sitting by the deathbed of his friend so it seems I must wait a little longer."

"You must be patient, Peter, but 'tis so good to spend this time with you."

He smiled fondly at his aunt. "Tell me about Roger's

wedding. It was being planned when I left. Where is your new daughter-in-law? I thought that she would accompany you to Dublin."

"Ah, t'was a sad business, Peter. I really liked his bride and he was smitten with her. I could tell. But she had a puppy." Aunt Margaret shook her head. "Roger couldn't tolerate her bringing it in the house so she broke off the engagement. *"You are choosing your dog over me!"* he yelled and she replied, *'Precisely.'* And then she walked out, just as we were about to sit down to dinner. Since then, Roger has been very difficult to live with. Even my trip here to Dublin caused trouble. He claimed he needed the carriage to go to the assizes, the regional courts, so I had to come in the pony cart."

"That's truly shocking, aunt. Why ever did Roger need to attend the assizes?"

"He didn't need to but he has decided that the current laws for poaching are too lax and wants to push for harsher penalties."

Peter shook his head. "I'm sorry, aunt. I do recall that Roger never cared for the people who worked his land. I tried to tell my uncle that he should treat them better also and now, it seems, his son is following in his footsteps."

"There's nothing you can do about it, Peter, but it's wonderful to have this visit with you," she said.

"When do you leave? Do you go tomorrow?" he asked.

"Yes, likely about ten in the morning for it will take some time to get the cart loaded up," she replied. "But I would like to know what transpires at the cathedral."

"Cross your fingers for me," he said.

"I'll do better than that, Peter. I'll say a prayer for you. After all you are dealing with the bishop."

"Good night then, aunt. We'll see each other in the morning." He kissed her on the cheek and left.

***

Dublin harbour was teeming with life in the early morning light. As Peter walked he looked for the ship he might be leaving on later. Ah, there she was. Crossing his fingers that things could be settled quickly he walked a little faster. Unfortunately, when he got to the cathedral the bishop was still unavailable. Peter retraced his steps, at a much slower pace this time, deep in thought. He couldn't leave Ireland without laying his hands on the marriage license but he couldn't escort Aunt Margaret back home and pick it up because he had to wait for his audience with the bishop. What to do? As he approached the Gibson Hotel he saw his aunt; Clooney was in tow and carrying a large bundle out of the door. Ah, the solution! So simple!

"Good morning, Aunt Margaret, I have a change of plans. May I speak to Clooney for a moment? Don't worry, aunt, this won't take long."

They walked up the street for a little ways. "Clooney I have a proposition for you," Peter said. "My aunt has my parent's marriage license in safekeeping at Glendalough and I don't want to trust such an important document to the mail coach. I cannot travel to Glendalough as I am still awaiting an audience with the Bishop. What if you brought it to me tomorrow, then you and I can both sail to England? It will get you away from Roger and provide evidence to my claim. If, however, I am not successful in becoming Master of Linden Hall, I promise to find you work in England. What do you say – are you willing to take a chance on me?"

Clooney's eyes lit up. "Right you are, gov! Anything to get away from his nibs. You'll pay my way to England?"

"Yes, Clooney, I'll pay your ship's passage and your stagecoach at the other end."

"Then I'm your man," Clooney said.

They walked back to his aunt and Peter explained.

"That will be so much faster for you." She looked so frail. "I am very glad you came, Peter, God be with you," she said reaching up to kiss his cheek. He was saddened because he knew this would likely be the last time he would see his aunt. Solemnly, he watched them drive down the main street of Dublin, then, just before they were out of sight, Clooney made a cocky wave giving Peter hope.

***

The next day Peter went back to the cathedral. He sat on the wooden bench and looked around him. The morning sun shone through an old stained glass window set high in the wall making the rich colours glow. It was a peaceful, beautiful place but his nerves were on edge. He tried to relax but knew he didn't have much time if he wanted to be on a ship bound for Liverpool as soon as Clooney retuned. A door opened. A man wearing a black cassock beckoned and Peter followed. He walked into a dark wood panelled room with a large desk covered with papers. Behind it sat an elderly man who looked exhausted. Peter bowed before him.

"Sit down my son, you wished to see me?"

"Yes, your worship. Thank you for giving me an interview. My name is Peter Trigan. My parents were married here, at Christ Church Cathedral, twenty-eight years ago and their marriage was recorded in your parish register. I need written proof of their wedding to take back to England. My right to inherit the title of Lord Berrington and the estate, which it entails, has been challenged.

Without proof of my parents' legal marriage I stand to lose everything."

"I see. I will compose a letter with my official seal but if your father purchased a license it would help with the proof you seek."

"They married in haste but yes, my father did purchase a license."

"Ah, good," the bishop said with a knowing smile. "I will prepare the letter you need. It will be ready for you upon the hour."

"I thank you from the bottom of my heart," Peter said, bowing deeply.

***

Peter went to the docks. With any luck he and Clooney would be sailing soon but right now there wasn't a ship in sight. His heart sank. What if his aunt's pony cart broke down? What if Clooney couldn't get away? What if Roger made difficulties for him? What if, what if? That night he slept badly.

The next morning he returned to the docks and couldn't believe his eyes. There stood the Merriweather, the self-same ship that had brought him over to Ireland five days ago. She must have arrived in the night. He spoke to the captain who was keeping an anxious eye on the weather, for a storm was brewing in the west.

"We leave on the tide. Mark you be here at dawn if you're sailing with us," the captain said.

Peter promptly paid for his own passage and Clooney's as well. Then he settled in to wait for Clooney. Finally, having taken the long way round so as to avoid meeting Roger as he returned from the assizes, Clooney arrived close to midnight. He reached into his pocket and, with a flourish and a grin, handed Peter a leather package.

"Good man! You have it. Well done, Clooney, thank you."

He took Clooney in the pub for a pint of ale and some pasties. As he was wolfing them down, Peter unwrapped the packet. Inside, were his parent's marriage license and a small leather pouch. He reached carefully into the pouch and pulled out a beautiful gold ring set with diamonds and a single ruby. There was a note; it read,

"*Dear Peter,*

This ring was your mother's. Perhaps you can find a young lady to wear it for you.

God Speed,

Your loving Aunt Margaret"

The next day Peter stood with Clooney on the bow of the Merriweather watching the city of Dublin recede on the horizon. He heaved a sigh of relief. He had overcome one obstacle. There were more ahead but he felt a surge of confidence. The future held so much promise. However, the captain had been right about a storm blowing in from the west; it caught them right in the middle of the Irish Sea. "Got your wish to go to sea, Clooney, but it's a good thing you didn't become a sailor," Peter said with a shake of his head as Clooney went back to feeding the fish for a third time!

Chapter Eight

Ruby and Caitlin made plans to take the midnight stagecoach because it was cheaper and there was less chance of discovery. But also because they would be well on their way before their absence was noticed. Caitlin needed somewhere to don her disguise and, since the Dabbley's had a small stable behind their town house, it was decided that it would be best to meet there at eleven o'clock.

After her aunt had gone to bed, Ruby changed into her plainest country clothes and crept up to the attic. She returned to her room and put on the hat and veil. Looking in the mirror she decided that her disguise was effective; only a close friend might recognize her. About to slip out the door, Ruby was conscience stricken. Her aunt would be so worried. She sat down at the escritoire and quickly penned a note.

"*Dear Aunt Ada,*

Thank you for everything but Lord Fenwick and the Season are not for me.

Much love,

Your niece, Ruby"

She propped the note on her pillow where the maid would be sure to find it. Then she crept down the hall carrying her bundle, walking slowly down the stairs so as to avoid the creaky ones. Before leaving she checked to ensure that she had put the rest of her money into the black beaded reticule that she would give Caitlin to carry.

Outside in the cool night air Ruby breathed deeply. She looked up the street, both ways and was glad to see it was deserted. Most party-goers had already arrived at their destination for the evening and it was far too early for those returning home to be on the road. She walked quickly down to the corner and heaved a sigh of relief when she was out of sight of her aunt's townhouse. Fortunately, the Dabbley's residence was only a few streets away and soon she slipped into their stables. Caitlin hadn't arrived. A horse whinnied. She froze, lest a stable boy appear, but no one did. Then she heard the door creak and Caitlin was there.

"Ruby?" she whispered.

"Over here, Caitlin," Ruby said hugging her. "Quick. Take off your dress. I'll help." In no time, Caitlin was wearing the black-trimmed underclothes and was about to slip off her old ones when Ruby stopped her. "Let's roll up your own chemise and petticoat so that they sit partially under your corset. It will make you look fatter so that you fill out my aunt's gown."

With some nervous giggling this was managed and Aunt Ada's dress was settled over it all.

"I feel like a stuffed sausage," Caitlin giggled.

"But now the dress fits just right. Quick. Put on the black hat and veil." Ruby stood back to look at the result. "Caitlin, you are transformed. No one would recognize you, least of all me." She thrust the reticule, with all their money, into Caitlin's hands. Then she rolled up Caitlin's old dress and tucked it under her arm. "Quickly, now. We must hurry. I think we may be able to hail a hackney carriage one street over, where it's busier, but first we must dispose of your dress."

They turned the corner and saw a hackney coming toward them. Ruby quickly pushed the bundled dress under a nearby hedge while Caitlin hailed the carriage. The driver stopped.

"Can you take us to the 'Swan with the Two Heads Inn' on Lad's Lane?" Ruby asked.

The coachman nodded and they climbed in.

***

An hour later a full-figured older woman in deep mourning, wearing a very good quality, albeit out-of-date, black gown and a hat with a heavy veil boarded a coach at the 'Swan with the Two Heads Inn'. She was accompanied by a young woman in half mourning judging by the black veil draped over her straw bonnet. They had the coach to themselves for a few minutes while the other passengers purchased their tickets.

"You look so convincing, Caitlin. You fit Aunt Ada's mourning clothes perfectly. She must have been plumper then because the padding we put around your waist doesn't make your hemline ride up. I found the clothes in an old trunk in the attic. I doubt that Aunt Ada will miss them but I did leave a note inside it saying I was just borrowing them."

"Good for you, Ruby. This disguise is perfect. Best of all, it hides my hair which always stands out."

"Be sure to keep your black lace mittens on, too. You don't have the hands of an old woman."

"I will, now what did you say my name was?"

"You are Lady Fenton and I am your niece, Miss Serena Fenton. We're bound for St. Swithin's. It is further than we need to travel but we don't want to give ourselves away – anyone searching for us will look for tickets bought to the village of Thornton."

"Oh how clever you are to think of that, Ruby. Did you have to pawn your mother's earrings?" Caitlin asked, her glance sympathetic.

"Yes. I did but perhaps your brother can redeem them for me someday? My maid had to guide me to the pawnshop and the stage coach station. I hope she'll keep our confidence. It's to her advantage otherwise she could get dismissed without a reference. Now tell me, before the others board. What transpired with your godparents?"

"I couldn't think of what to do. Then I remembered that betrothals are often announced at balls and the Cunningham's ball is this Saturday. I told Dulsin that I needed a few days to consider his kind offer, that I would give him an answer on the morning of the ball. Lady Sally took my announcement to mean that of course I would accept and started planning what I should wear and even offered some of her jewellery. Dulsin seemed very pleased and went off to have a drink with Lord Dabbley."

Before she could finish, a middle aged couple got into the coach. It was a Mrs. Bucket and her husband. They had a store in the village of Thornton, close to Thorncroft Hall and she was the worst village gossip. Sure enough, Mrs. Bucket started questioning Ruby as soon as the carriage started moving. With dread, Ruby answered very carefully, realizing that she would be very lucky indeed if Mrs. Bucket didn't recognize her.

"Where are you travelling to?" the busybody asked.

Without waiting for a reply she then added, "We're headed to Thornton in Kent."

"We're going to St. Swithin's," Ruby said.

"So it must be a close relative of yours who's passed?" Mrs. Bucket asked.

"Yes, my sister's brother-in-law. It was all was very sudden. She can't speak of it," she murmured as she reached out to clasp the black-gloved hand of 'Lady Fenton' beside her.

"Ah, that's why you're not in full mourning yourself then. Yes. It's very sad I'm sure. But you look familiar somehow. Where are you from?"

Ruby gave the name of a village on the far side of London. Would the woman never stop her interrogations? But as if on cue, 'Lady Fenton' started crying and her 'niece' turned away to give comfort.

Fortunately Mrs. Bucket was curious about everyone and now proceeded to pepper the old lady sitting across from her with questions. As the hours passed Mrs. Bucket dozed off. But the closer they came to the village of Thornton, the more Ruby struggled with a dilemma. If they got off there, Mrs. Bucket would be sure to find out where they were headed. But if they stayed on the coach until St. Swithin's, to which they had paid the fare, they would have a very long walk home.

Eventually, Ruby dozed off herself as the night progressed. She awoke as they drove into St. Swithin's and the Buckets were no longer on the stagecoach. She looked at Caitlin who had slept soundly leaning on her shoulder all night while she herself had been awake for hours listening to the coachman calling out the names of the villages they passed. She shook Caitlin awake.

"Where are we?" Caitlin asked rubbing her eyes with difficulty, from under the veil.

"St. Swithin's, and we have a long walk ahead of us. Come, let's get out of the coach."

Caitlin yawned. "I'm hungry."

"We'll have breakfast once we get to my father's. But just listen to the birds singing. The sun is coming out and the air is so fresh. It is so peaceful in the countryside. Hurry up now. We must be on our way." She took Caitlin by the arm and led the way through the village and onto the open road. As soon as they were out of sight from the village she turned off onto a path she remembered. It cut across the fields and would shorten their long walk by a good half hour. Thankfully, they met no one since it was still very early in the day.

Thorncroft Hall appeared in the distance, finally. With relief, they reached the paddock just as Ruby's father was tightening the stirrups on his horse before going out for a morning ride as was his custom.

"Father!" Ruby called as she ran towards him pulling off her hat and concealing black veil. "It's me, Ruby."

"Daughter! What is the meaning of this? What are you doing here? And who is that woman with you?"

"This is my friend, Caitlin Trigan. We've run away from London together. Here Caitlin, take off your veil and hat." Caitlin did so, showing her red hair and sweet young face. She curtseyed to Sir Roderick.

"You'd best come in then. I'm sure there's a long story to tell," he said gruffly.

"Yes, father and we're also very hungry. We haven't broken our fast yet."

"Very well. Annie will make you some breakfast while

you get out of those ridiculous clothes. Then, Ruby, you and I will talk."

Wary of his stern tone, she said, "Yes, father, but aren't you even a little glad to see me?"

"You know I am but that's not the point, daughter," he said turning away.

Ruby took Caitlin up to her room and found them some clothes to change into. Then, they sat down to Annie's hearty breakfast of fresh farm eggs and bacon all washed down with strong tea, no one to question their manners. Ruby was just slathering more jam on her buttered bread when the butler interrupted them.

"Sir Roderick is expecting you in the library, miss."

Ruby fortified herself with another bite of bread and wiped her hands on the linen napkin. After giving Caitlin what she hoped was a reassuring look she made her way to the library. She took a deep breath and opened the door.

"Come in, daughter. I've been waiting to speak to you," he said, his tone serious. "How could you have been so foolhardy as to run away by yourselves and take an overnight stage coach at that? Don't you realize what could have happened to you? You and your friend could have been kidnapped, or suffered a fate worse than death. I thought I raised you to have more sense, my girl."

"I'm very sorry, father. I really tried. Caitlin did, too, but London is not for everyone. The whole marriage mart is sickening. Men court their future wives as they're arranging to keep mistresses on the side. Aunt Ada was very good to me but she was pushing me to marry Lord Fenwick, a boring widower with a house on the outskirts of London. I don't want to live in that smelly place with daily smog."

"So that's it? Are you sure there isn't anything you've forgotten to tell me?" Her father gave her a piercing look.

Could he know about Lord Sayward? No, it wasn't possible. "No, that's all, father. Except I should write to Aunt Ada, I expect she is likely worried about me. I don't want to marry, father. I want to live here in the country and look after you."

"Yes. I think you should write Ada – immediately – but the issue here is your future, daughter. Once I'm gone this estate passes to your brother, Matthew. When he marries his wife will be the lady of Thorncroft Hall, not you. I want you to have a home of your own, and babes of your own. If you stay here you will end up being little more than a nursemaid to your nieces and nephews. That's not all I'd hoped for you, Ruby. That's why I sent you to London." He turned his back on her to look out the window then said over his shoulder, "And what about your friend, Caitlin, is it?"

"She was being pressured to accept a betrothal from a Lord Dulsin. She couldn't stand for him to even touch her, yet her godmother said it was an excellent match. She doesn't want to marry either. She wants to study the harp. Her brother, Lord Berrington, has inherited Linden Hall. He drove me home in our tilbury, when I twisted my ankle just before I left for London. You met him, remember father? When he returns to Linden Hall Caitlin plans to stay with him."

"Ah yes, I remember. Very well, we will leave it as is for now but I don't want you to have anything to do with him. As I told you before, I don't like the Irish."

Chapter Nine

Peter and Clooney arrived in Liverpool the next morning, despite the storm, and took a mail coach to London; it cost more but made better time. In London they went straight to the Dabbley's townhouse. Peter made sure that Clooney was settled then went in search of Lord Dabbley.

"You're back. Come in come in. Did you get the proof you need?" Lord Dabbley asked, waving him into the library.

"Yes. I believe so. I have a letter from the bishop with his official seal and I have my parents' marriage license from 1790."

"Very good. We must have your case reviewed as soon as possible. In fact I will send a note to my friend, Lord Carrington, right away. He will know how best to proceed."

He scribbled quickly, folded the paper, sealed it with wax and stamped it with his personal insignia. He tugged the bell pull and when his butler arrived within seconds he asked that it be sent post haste.

"Now, would you care for a brandy?" Lord Dabbley asked.

"Yes. I think I need one. It has been an eventful week. I've brought a young man back with me whom I hope to employ at Linden Hall. He is downstairs now but it's a long story so I'd best start at the beginning..."

He sat down by the hearth with his lordship and began.

***

The next day at breakfast Lord Dabbley received a missive. He read aloud to Peter, carefully. "This is from my friend, Carrington. He says the best approach would be to ask for a private audience with the Lord Chancellor. If he believes you have sufficient proof it need go no further as he can make a judgement on the case himself."

"I see. Where do I find the Lord Chancellor?" Peter asked.

"My man will take you there as soon as you've eaten."

"I've just lost my appetite."

"Believe me. You'd best eat up as you may have a long wait," Lord Dabbley warned.

"In that case I'll have some sausages and bacon." Peter said piling up his plate.

The door opened and Lady Dabbley came into the breakfast room. "Peter! I missed your arrival last night, welcome back. I'm so glad you're here. Have you heard from Caitlin?"

"No, but then I didn't expect to. She's here with you, isn't she?"

"No. That's just it. I am afraid she isn't, she's gone! Just vanished at about the same time as you left for Dublin. We have no idea where she might be. I hoped she had been in touch with you, or even gone to Ireland with you, I'm beside myself with worry." Lady Dabbley said her voice very strained.

"But that's terrible! Was she upset about anything?" Peter asked.

Lord and Lady Dabbley exchanged a look. Then Dabbley cleared his throat. "He has a right to know, my dear." He turned to Peter. "We were in the process of announcing her betrothal to Lord Dulsin. It is a good match but when she seemed reluctant, we applied some gentle pressure. And the next thing you know she's run away. We don't know any more than that. I'm sorry."

"But surely you've spoken to some of her friends?" Peter asked.

"Well that's just it. She didn't seem to have any." Lady Dabbley said, "Although, there was that young lady from Kent, Ruby. I'm not sure of her last name."

"You mean Miss Gillingham?"

"Yes, that's it!" she replied, eagerly. "She was staying with her aunt, Lady Paxton. I'll contact her right away."

***

Peter was ready to drop everything to hunt for his sister but Lord Dabbley was of a different mind; he was adamant that Peter first address the issue of his inheritance. "No, young man. This simply cannot wait. Go to the Lord Chancellor today. He will likely make you wait for an answer and you can put that time to good use looking for Caitlin. Also you will have an easier time getting help if you have a title. That is simply a fact of life. If a Peter Trigan asks for help he may eventually get it but if Lord Berrington asks for the same, assistance will be forthcoming much sooner."

Peter had to agree and so he went to the government offices.

After waiting for three hours, Peter was at last ushered in to see the Lord Chancellor. He stated his case and handed over the documents obtained in Ireland. His lordship read them carefully, then looked up, his white wig having slid so low on his forehead that it almost rested on his eyebrows.

"These papers are in order. But the question of inheritance of an English title also depends on your nationality. Was your father an Englishman, Mr. Trigan?"

"Yes, my lord," Peter answered.

"Where was he born?"

"My father was born here in London, milord and –"

"—What year and where was he baptised?" the chancellor cut him off.

"1765, milord, at the church of St Marylebone," Peter added.

"I will send a clerk to verify this. If what you say is true, then the title is yours. Even if you, yourself, were born in Ireland a child takes the nationality of the father. You will be notified of my final verdict as soon as the parish records are checked. Good day, young man."

Peter bowed deeply and was escorted out of the room.

***

As soon as he left the Chancellery, Peter hired a hackney carriage to Mayfair where Lady Paxton lived. When he arrived at Crescent Street, the butler met him at the door.

"Please tell her ladyship that Lord Berrington wishes to speak with her," He felt a little deceptive using the title because it was still being challenged but Lady Paxton would recognize the name Berrington from the bouquets he had sent.

The butler came back, immediately. "This way, milord."

Berrington was shown into a drawing room decorated in an old-fashioned style that nevertheless spoke of wealth. A cream and mauve Aubusson carpet covered the floor in front of a blazing fire. Maroon velvet drapes were partially drawn against the early evening dusk. An older lady anxiously paced before the hearth. She paused upon Peter's entrance and looked at him, a question clearly on her lips.

"Lord Berrington, you sent flowers to my niece?"

"Yes, my lady," he replied. "I hope she is well?"

"Well, that's just it. I don't know. I had hoped you might know where she is," she said twisting her clasped hands together. "Please, do sit." She indicated a maroon settee behind him and took a seat by the fire.

"I had no idea Miss Gillingham was not with you, milady. Actually, I came to ask if she knew where my sister, Caitlin, might be. While I was away in Dublin, she vanished. About a week ago according to her godparents, Lord and Lady Dabbley," he said.

"But that is about the same time Ruby disappeared."

"Could they have run away together?" Peter said thinking out loud.

Lady Paxton stared at him. "Where could they go? Two young girls alone?" She looked as if she were ready to cry.

"Is it possible that they have gone to Kent, to Miss Gillingham's home, Thorncroft Hall?"

"But how? With no money?" she asked.

"A stage coach doesn't cost that much. Have you questioned your servants? Perhaps one of them might know something."

"Yes I did, but no one admitted to knowing anything. Here is the letter my niece left." She picked up the missive and handed it to him.

Berrington read it carefully. "It sounds to me as if Miss Gillingham would rather be in the country than in the London Season. Have you written to her father?"

"No. Not yet. I don't know what to write, how to explain to my brother. I keep hoping I won't have to, keep hoping Ruby will come back. I feel that I have failed her in some way."

"I will go to the 'Swan with Two Heads'. It is the staging post for travel between here and Kent. Perhaps someone will remember seeing two girls getting on alone last week."

"Please let me know what you find out. I beg you," she said.

"I will my lady. Now I must go. If you need anything further, I'm staying with Lord and Lady Dabbley on South Audley Street." He bowed and was on his way.

Peter took the hackney to the 'Swan with Two Heads' but had little success. As far as anyone could recall, the only two women travelling together appeared to be related; the elder had been in complete mourning, while the other wore half mourning. No one remembered a redhead. Caitlin would have been noticed.

Exasperated, Peter took the hackney to Lord Dabbley's and arrived just in time for dinner. Since guests were expected, Dabbley took Peter aside for a private conversation in the library.

"So how did you make out with the Lord Chancellor and any news of Caitlin?"

After explaining what had transpired regarding his claim he continued, "Since speaking with Lady Paxton, I think the two girls may have run away together. It's merely a hunch at this point. I must travel to Kent to gain proof but I can't go until my title is secure." He heaved a sigh of frustration.

"I understand," Lord Dabbley said. "And I, too, am concerned about my godchild. But come have dinner with us. I will continue to introduce you as Berrington until it's proved otherwise – and I really doubt it will be."

***

Peter did not know what to do the next day. He considered sending a note to Lady Paxton but had nothing to report yet. The more he thought about it, the more he became convinced that the two women dressed in mourning clothes, who had boarded the stage coach for Kent, were the missing girls. What better disguise for his sister, Caitlin? However, he could do nothing until his title was cleared.

In efforts to distract himself, Peter went to see about the goods he had ordered for Linden Hall. Everything was in order but why pay for the items and the shipping if he might lose the right to live there? Best to wait for news before taking action on that, better to return to the Dabbley's where he could take advantage of the well-stocked shelves in their library. He found a copy of Debrett's and settled into a comfy chair by the fire to trace his elusive title. The book went back to the time of Henry VIII. Before he got very far in his research, news from the Chancellery Office arrived; Peter was to present himself at ten o' clock the next morning at which time he would meet with the Lord Chancellor.

Peter didn't sleep well that night. His future seemed clearly divided. Either he would be exonerated, become Lord Berrington of Linden Hall with all the privileges associated with that station in life, or he would be back at Oxford, a penniless student with a modest future in a law office. He thought his claim was irrefutable but perhaps the Lord Chancellor had found a loophole? He hoped not.

He was at the Chancellery Office an hour early the next day. At ten o'clock, precisely, he was ushered into the stately office. The Lord Chancellor stood up as Peter entered.

"Congratulations, Lord Berrington," he said with a smile. "The title is yours and I may add – the fact that you acted promptly was in your favour because lesser claimants were applying pressure."

"Thank you, my lord, I appreciate your assistance," he said. He bowed before being quickly ushered out of the room. Clearly, the Lord Chancellor was a very busy man.

Peter almost skipped down the marble steps to the street. So the vultures had been circling, had they, or perhaps just one vulture, in particular? He smiled with satisfaction. He hired a hackney cab and went to settle his accounts and pay for the delivery of his shipment of goods to Linden Hall. Then, since his right to be there had now been confirmed, he decided to drop in at Boodles men's club. As he was entering the club someone called his name.

"Congratulations, Lord Berrington!" Lord Dabbley said as he came up to him and patted him on the shoulder.

"Why, thank you, my lord. But how did you know? I only just found out myself," Berrington said with a laugh.

"The Morning Post, my boy. It carried an announcement. Here. Read it for yourself." He thrust the paper into Peter's hand. They entered Boodles and sat down to join some of his lordship's cronies. When they heard his news they called for their drinks to be charged again and raised their glasses. "To Lord Berrington of Linden Hall!" they cried.

Peter looked around and caught the eye of Lord Sayward who was sitting to one side with a furious expression on his face. He had heard the toasts no doubt. But then Berrington realized that Sayward had another reason for frowning. Ellington was standing over him brandishing a paper under his nose. He leaned forward to catch their conversation.

"You owe me twenty pounds, your lordship. We had a bet and you lost. Your little love nest sits empty to this day."

Sayward scribbled a promissory note and handed it to the grinning man. Then he stood up and left the room glaring at Berrington as he passed him.

Berrington smiled, sighed, sat back and relaxed. He looked around the cozy oak panelled room with its aroma of imported cigars. The other men resumed their former conversations. It felt good to be accepted into this elite male enclave. He turned to Lord Dabbley. "I will be leaving tomorrow for Kent. I need to track down Caitlin as soon as can be," he said.

"I understand. Please let me know what you discover. Lady Dabbley is very worried also."

***

Early the next morning Berrington and Clooney were at the 'Swan with the Two Heads' to catch the mail coach which would get them to Kent by afternoon. Berrington was eager to get back to Linden Hall and begin his search for Caitlin. Judging by the expression on Clooney's face he was happy to be leaving London too. There were no seats left inside the coach so they sat outside, on the roof.

"Nice view from here," Berrington said.

"And fresh air, at last." Clooney replied. "That place stank!"

"Aye. I'd hate to live in London all year round. Can you imagine it on a warm summer day? I think you'll like

Linden Hall better, Clooney. It's out in the green countryside with fields and woodland."

"So, you're now the rightful master?" Clooney asked.

"Yes. That's right, I am. Finally."

When the stage stagecoach dropped them off at the village of Thornton they hired two horses and made the rest of the journey on horseback. When they arrived at Linden Hall, Mrs. Banbury gave them a warm welcome and a simple, filling supper. "I think you'll have to sleep in the hayloft tonight, Clooney but we'll sort out your accommodations in the next few days."

"To be sure I've done it before, plenty of times, and I like the smell of hay!" he laughed.

Berrington requested hot water to bathe and asked Mrs. Banbury to iron a shirt for him. He had to look presentable when he went to Thorncroft Hall in the morning. He needed to make a good impression for Ruby's father had not been too friendly.

Chapter Ten

In the morning Berrington rode over to Thorncroft Hall not knowing what to expect. Were the girls there? If they weren't he didn't know where he would look next. He dismounted and knocked on the door.

"Lord Berrington come to speak with Sir Roderick," he said to the butler.

The butler returned in moments, "Please follow me," he said.

Berrington entered the library and bowed. Sir Roderick did not rise to greet him nor did he utter a word.

"Good day to you sir," Berrington began. "I am here to ask if you may know the whereabouts of my sister, Caitlin Trigan. She met your daughter, Miss Gillingham in London I believe. Now my sister has gone missing." He waited for Sir Roderick to speak. When the silence continued he added, "She has red, er... auburn hair."

"Yes, she's here. She came home with Ruby last week." He tugged a bell pull. "Tell Miss Trigan to come down," he said but still omitted to offer Berrington a seat. The door opened and Caitlin walked in. She took one look at Peter, ran into his arms and promptly burst into tears.

"You came, I was hoping you would but I didn't know how to get in touch with you," she said.

"You had me worried, Cait. Very worried."

"I'm sorry, Peter, I really am – but I won't go back to London." She looked at him warily.

"I see. But how about Linden Hall?" he asked.

"Oh, yes please! I'd love to see your new home," she said breaking into a big smile.

Just then Ruby ran into the room.

"Berrington!" she said happily. "Where did you come from?"

"From London, as I gather you did too," he said.

She looked so relaxed and happy, unlike her London self.

Sir Roderick cleared his throat. "It appears that you have found your sister, milord, and I'm sure you're anxious to take her home now."

"Yes, sir, I have and I do. And I wish to thank you for taking care of her." He turned to Caitlin. "Please get your things. We should be on our way."

"Of course, but I didn't bring much." She looked in confusion from him to Ruby to Sir Roderick then scurried from the room.

Berrington could see that he wasn't welcome. He would have to do something about that later. But today there was one thing he wanted to know before he left. He looked at Ruby. "Did you and Caitlin dress in mourning clothes for your journey on the stagecoach?"

"Yes. How did you know?" Ruby asked.

"Just a shrewd guess," he answered as Caitlin came back

carrying a small bundle. She hugged Ruby. Berrington bowed a second time and they left Thorncroft Hall.

"I'm afraid you'll have to ride pillion, Cait," Berrington said lifting her up behind his saddle.

"I'd like that," she said, hugging him around his waist as they trotted down the drive.

***

When they got back to Linden Hall Mrs. Banbury settled Caitlin by the fire with a pot of tea while she went upstairs to organize one of the rooms and put new linens on the bed. Berrington came and sat down beside her.

"So Cait, tell me, what happened in London? I thought you liked Lady Sally."

"I do, but I didn't like the husband she'd picked out for me. I don't want to marry, Peter. I just want to study the harp. Can I live here with you?"

"You can stay here, on one condition. You must promise never to do anything so foolhardy again – two young girls unprotected travelling alone in the night was foolhardy. You could have vanished and I would have never known what had become of you. I promised Mother I'd look after you, Cait." He glared at her a little longer and then relented. "Where is your harp, by the way?"

"I had to leave it at the Dabbley's when we ran away. I should write them and apologize."

"Yes. Lord and Lady Dabbley were most worried and you can also ask them to keep your harp until the next time I go to London."

***

Thorncroft Hall seemed unusually quiet to Ruby without the Caitlin. So, one day she decided to visit her old friend, Penelope. Yes, she'd gone over once with Caitlin so that her friends could meet but she and

Penelope were overdue for a good heart-to-heart, just the two of them. She found Penelope in the morning room knitting.

"Ruby! What a lovely surprise!" she said jumping up to give her a hug. "Is Caitlin with you?"

"No. She's gone to live with her brother, Berrington," Ruby said.

"So he's back. Were you glad to see him?"

"I was but my father wasn't. He doesn't want me to have anything to do with him. But since I plan to stay friends with Caitlin I'm can't avoid going to Linden Hall."

"Has your father ever explained why he doesn't like the Irish?"

"No, but it's not that unusual. Is it?"

"Perhaps not but maybe you could get him to see that he's being unreasonable," Penelope said as she held up her knitting. "Look what I'm making."

"It's a tiny sweater – a baby sweater! Penelope – are you? Are you with child?" Ruby asked, hardly able to believe her eyes.

"Yes. I am. I had been hoping that was the case and now I'm sure." She beamed at Ruby. "And Jonathan is as delighted, as I am, so we're setting up our nursery."

"That's wonderful news, Penelope. I'm really happy for you."

"Thank you. Aunt Felicity is in heaven. She's knitting more than I am. I think this
child is going to have baby sweaters by the dozens."

***

As Ruby drove the tilbury home she realized that Penelope's news had made her feel a little left out. For so long she had dreamt of marrying Crispin of being Lady Sayward and in that dream babies would have swiftly followed. Now that was not to be. In fact, if she were being honest with herself, she now realised that she didn't want him anywhere in her life at all. But she would like a home of her own, and like Penelope, a loving husband and babies, too. It would be her dream come true. But she also wanted the freedom to go into her own kitchen and bake if she so chose. What man would allow her to do that, unless he was a commoner? However, that wouldn't please her father. Life was so complicated.

There was Berrington, she liked being in his company. He made her feel desirable in a ladylike way, the way he picked her up as if she were as light as thistledown, the way he had looked at her the night they so daringly waltzed together on the moonlit terrace. For reasons unknown, her father was being stubborn about the fact that Peter was Irish. But wait – how could he have inherited an English title if he were Irish? This bore further investigation.

Ruby settled into the pattern of her previous country life. She took long walks. She consulted with Annie, the cook, about menus and made sure that there was always enough extra food for her to take to the elderly and shut-ins. She made a weekly trip to the market in Thornton and began to run into Berrington. Whenever she was in the village he always seemed to be there and he always made a point of stopping to chat.

"Good day, Miss Gillingham. It's lovely to see you looking so well," he said, bowing as best he could on horseback.

"Thank you, milord. Country life agrees with me," she answered thinking that it agreed with him too. She couldn't help but notice his muscular body revealed by his snug fitting buckskin breeches. He was having trouble making his energetic young stallion hold still, it wanted its head but Berrington quietly but firmly got it under control. Ruby swallowed, noticing how virile yet gentle he was. "How is Caitlin?" she asked as she reached up to pat his horse on the nose.

The stallion whinnied in appreciation of her attention. Berrington felt the same but had the presence of mind to answer. "She's well but feeling very lost without her harp. You should come visit her. She would love to see you and you can see all the improvements I've made to Linden Hall."

"I will, milord. I promise. Tell Caitlin I'm thinking of her." She bobbed a curtsey and walked on as Berrington let his horse have its head.

Ruby wanted to visit Caitlin but if her father found out she'd gone to Linden Hall, there would be trouble. She had promised herself that she wouldn't let her father stop her from doing things she wanted to do – as long as they were harmless – but she would rather not upset him if possible. Perhaps if she went when he was busy, her visits could be kept secret?

On a day when she knew her father would be home late, she had Poppy tacked up with her side-saddle then rode over to Linden Hall. The linden trees along the drive were beginning to lose their leaves, it was that time of year, but she remembered their heady perfume the previous spring. As she approached the mansion its gabled roof peeked out of the surrounding greenery atop its faded rosy brick exterior. A circular drive led up to the front entrance, which framed a heavy wooden door carved with an intricate design of linden leaves.

Caitlin ran out to greet her and not waiting for a groom to help her dismount, Ruby slid elegantly to the ground. "However did you do that?' Caitlin asked. "I'm not good with horses. I always hope someone will drive me, if I have to go somewhere."

"Poppy is a sweet tempered horse. You wouldn't need to be afraid if she was yours." She turned to look up at the house. "So this is Linden Hall, restored to its former glory. I love the old brick work."

"Wait until you come inside, I'll show you more." Caitlin led the way into the great hall which had oak panelling and plaster walls painted a fresh cream colour. A fire burned in the hearth and a dog slept in front of it. He came forward to see who had arrived, sniffing Ruby's hand.

"I think this would be a good place for my harp," Caitlin said indicating a corner to one side. But come through into the morning room." Just off the hall was a smaller, cozier room. It had brass firedogs and a round table with some comfortable chairs. "It gets the best morning light, thus its name. I like to read or write letters here. Now follow me and I'll show you my bedroom." She took Ruby up a polished staircase, off the main hall, which creaked at almost every step. Caitlin giggled. "I don't think a burglar would stand a chance. We would hear him both coming and going."

Caitlin's room was at the end of the passageway. It had curtains and a half tester bed done up in yellow and white chintz, a dresser which doubled as a washstand and a chair. "Come see the best part," she said indicating a window, which looked down on a courtyard. An old stone angel stood centered in a small ornamental pool and the remains of dried flowers from the previous summer lay in the circular bed around it. In the distance you could see a pasture with two horses grazing.

"Yes. What a lovely view," Ruby said. "I'm sure you saw

nothing so picturesque out of your bedroom window in London."

They went back to the morning room and were having tea when Ruby remembered a question that had been troubling her. "Caitlin, I know you grew up in Ireland but are you and your brother Irish or English?" she asked.

"We're English. Since both of our parents were English it doesn't matter where we were born," Caitlin replied.

"Just as I thought," Ruby said. "But it seems it does makes a difference to some people."

"Really? To whom?" Caitlin asked.

"To my father, for one, but please don't worry. It's not your concern. However, if I am to get back to Thorncroft before him, I should leave."

"Well if you must, but do come again soon. Peter will be sorry to have missed you."

"Peter? Oh you mean Berrington."

"Yes. I can't get used to using his title," Caitlin replied.

A groom tossed Ruby up into the saddle and Poppy was trotting down the drive when she met Berrington. He sketched her a bow in the saddle.

"You're leaving," he said in dismay. "I would be honoured if you would stay for supper."

"Thank you but I have to be home shortly. Perhaps I can come another day. You have done wonders with Linden Hall though."

"Thank you. There is more to do but it takes time. I'll ride back with you, then we can talk."

"No, no. I'll be fine. You forget that I've grown up here – and it's still daylight."

But Berrington was determined to make sure she got home safely so she stopped protesting. Maybe her father really would get home late after all?

"Why did you have to go to Ireland? Caitlin said it had something to do with your title?"

"Yes, it was. My right to inherit the title and the entailed property, Linden Hall, was challenged so I had to get proof of my parents' legal marriage. Since they eloped and were married in Dublin, it meant I had to go to Ireland and time was of the essence. I wanted to tell you but truly I could not stop. I had to get on the next boat for Dublin."

"How terrible. Do you know who made the challenge?"

"Yes. It was Lord Sayward."

"Oh! He's horrid! I know from experience how despicable he is," she said.

"I couldn't agree with you more. But my claim is resolved and my title is secure."

They were within sight of Thorncroft Hall so Ruby stopped and turned to Berrington.

"Thank you for escorting me home. That was kind of you. Good day."

He opened his mouth to object but realized that she didn't want him to come any further. If he wanted to court her he would have to address this and the sooner the better. "Good bye then, Miss Gillingham. It was a pleasure to see you." He took her gloved hand and kissed it but didn't release it. "Do you remember when we danced the waltz together?"

"Yes. I do," she replied, all at once a little breathless.

"Perhaps again someday?" he asked with a hope in his eyes.

"That would be lovely,' she replied. "But I really must go now." She withdrew her hand from his reluctantly and he turned his horse away but continued to look back at her.

Chapter Eleven

Ruby rode up to the house with a nervous feeling in the pit of her stomach. She had spent longer at Linden Hall than expected and she was almost certain that her father was back, which meant he might have seen her riding up the road with Berrington. She left her horse in the stable and entered the house. Stanson was waiting for her in the front hall. "Your father wishes to speak with you in the library, miss," he said.

"Thank you, Stanson," Ruby said. She opened the library door and walked in. Her father stood in front of the fireplace. His face was beet red. It was as she had feared.

"Did I not tell you explicitly that I didn't want you to have anything to do with that Irishman?"

"Yes, father. You did. But I didn't go to see him. I went to visit his sister, Caitlin. He arrived as I was leaving and insisted on escorting me home. What is the harm in that?"

"I don't want you anywhere near him," he said. "And if I have to lock you in your room so be it."

"Why, father? You haven't given me a single good reason – excepting that you don't like the Irish. Why is that, father? What do you have against the Irish, or against him? Because I am willing to obey you if you give me a good reason but, so far, you haven't." She waited. Unusually, her father seemed at a loss for words. "I'll eat supper in my room, father," she said stonily and she left the library.

On her way through the front hallway she noticed a letter waiting for her, sitting on the silver salver. When Ruby got to her bedroom, she looked at the envelope in her hand. The only person who could be writing her from London was Aunt Ada. She took a deep breath and broke the wax seal. With some trepidation she slowly unfolded the letter.

"*Dear Ruby,*

Thank God you're safe, child! Do you know how many sleepless nights you're caused me? There was no need to run away just because you didn't care for Lord Fenwick. We would have found you someone else eventually.

I find it interesting that Lord Berrington is still in your life. He did seem to have a tendre for you. But you need to get your father to tell you about his sweetheart, the one who eloped to Ireland. Then you will understand why he dislikes the Irish so.

I would be happy to have you return to me in London. You left all your pretty dresses here.

Love

Your Aunt Ada"

Now wasn't that interesting? Yes, she would question her father in the morning.

***

Ruby found her father absorbed in an equestrian newsletter as he ate his oatmeal when she went downstairs to breakfast. "Good morning, father," she said sitting down. He looked up and just nodded. They ate in silence but as he rose from the table she spoke up. "I had a letter from Aunt Ada. She said that I should ask you to tell me about your sweetheart, the one who eloped with an Irishman. She said that only then would I understand your feelings about the Irish."

Lord Roderick's face flushed a deep red. "Ada had no business telling you that. It has nothing to do with you," he sputtered.

"I beg to differ, father. Your life influences mine so I feel I have a right to know our family history."

"She never became part of our family," he said turning his back to her.

"What was her name, father?"

"Dorothy."

"And how did you meet?"

"At a county fair, here in Thornton. She had such a sweet smile. Her father was interested in a colt we had and she drove over with him, to see it. After that we would meet on market days in town. I'd count the hours until I'd see her again. Eventually I approached her father asking for permission to court her. She was only seventeen, so her father said to wait a year and then I'd be welcome."

"But what happened, father," Ruby coaxed. This was fascinating.

"Well these Irishmen came to town, a father and son. They were buying horses for an estate in Ireland. Dorothy's father had an excellent breed of horses. The negotiations stretched on and during that time Dorothy never seemed to be in the marketplace. When they left Dorothy had changed. She was still friendly but no longer had that special way of looking at me when we spoke.

"The next thing I knew the village was buzzing with the news. Dorothy Sarton had vanished, eloped with the young Irishman. I never saw her again. I blamed him for stealing her away from me while I waited for her to grow up." Ruby's father turned and looked at Ruby. She saw the bleak look in his eyes.

"But then you met Matthew's mother," she prompted. "Didn't you love her?"

"Yes, I did. But you never forget your first love, even when life moves on."

Ruby could attest to that. It still hurt to think of Crispin. But now there was Berrington and she realized her feelings for him had deepened.

She looked out her window, a few days later, and saw Berrington riding up to their front door. Oh dear. Her father would not be pleased. She ran downstairs and before the butler could announce him, Ruby entered the library where her father was sitting at his desk. She cleared her throat. "Excuse me, father, but Lord Berrington is here to see you." As her father opened his mouth to protest, Ruby held up her hand. "Please father, hear me out. There is something you should know about him. He's not Irish. He is English."

"That's not possible. You can hear it in his speech. He is Irish!" her father said emphatically.

"Please, do let him explain it to you, father. He was a good friend to me in London when I needed one."

"A friend, you say?" Her father gave her a suspicious look.

"Yes. He was more trustworthy than many of the aristocrats I met. As soon as they found out that my mother was not a lady, I became merely a woman to proposition."

"Did this happen to you, daughter?"

Ruby nodded. "But it wasn't Berrington. He has always treated me with respect."

"Very well. You may invite him in. But don't expect me to welcome him with open arms."

"Just offer country hospitality, father. That's all I ask," Ruby said smiling.

Berrington entered the library and bowed deeply to both Ruby and her father. Her father sketched a semblance of a bow then looked at Berrington without smiling.

"My daughter insists that you are English. Explain to me, if you will, how this can be when you speak with an Irish accent," he said.

"Of course, sir. My parents were both English but yes, I did grow up in Glendalough, Ireland, which is why I speak the way I do. Later, I went to Oxford to study law, being a second son. My claim to Linden Hall, and the title which accompanies it, have just been confirmed by the Lord Chancellor in London."

"I see. Very well, young man. Sit down. Tell me. What is the state of Linden Hall at the moment? It stood empty far too long."

"I am making improvements to the buildings, step by step and have enlisted help with the running of the estate but I do need to acquire some more horses. I understand that your bloodstock is greatly valued within the county. Would you have any for sale?" Berrington asked with feigned guilelessness.

"Yes. It so happens I do," replied Sir Roderick, happy to have been presented with a means to make amends. "Shall we go out to the paddock? I can show you what I have."

As they left the house, Ruby heaved a sigh of relief. That had actually gone quite well. Perhaps now she could visit

Caitlin and see more of Berrington without upsetting her father?

Over the next few weeks Ruby made two trips to Linden Hall and once Berrington even brought Caitlin to see her.

"You are going to have to learn how to ride, Caitlin. It would make visiting so much easier," Ruby said.

"I used to ride but I've been afraid of horses since my fall a year ago. Anyway I rather think Peter had an ulterior motive for driving me here," Caitlin replied winking at Ruby.

That night as they sat down to dinner, her father cleared his throat a few times before speaking. "Young Berrington came to see me today. I think you will be pleased to know that I gave him permission to court you."

"Oh thank you, father. I do like him." Ruby smiled. She had been running into Berrington more and more frequently when she went to town and he often made her blush with his compliments.

***

On a crisp, sunny day in December with just a dusting of snow on the ground, Ruby rode out to Linden Hall but stopped near the pool where she and Berrington had first met. Their first meeting was imprinted in her memory; his vivid blue eyes, the musical lilt of his speech, his melting smile. Then she replayed their waltz on the terrace in the moonlight and her heart beat a little faster. It all fell into place. She loved Berrington. Yes! But what if he didn't share her feelings?

Raindrops on the bare bushes had frozen into crystals of ice, which sparkled and gleamed in the sun. A few small birds twittered and then a movement in the bushes caught her eye. There stood Berrington as if he had been waiting for her.

"What are you doing here?" she asked.

"Waiting for you. I knew you were coming to see Cait."

"But why meet me here?"

"I wanted a few moments of privacy – without Caitlin listening behind the door." He dropped to one knee in the snow and taking her hand said, "My dear Miss Gillingham will you do me the great honour of becoming my wife?"

"Oh yes, yes!" Ruby exclaimed. "But do get up. The ground is like ice. And I have a confession to make. I'm not quite a lady. My mother was a cook at Thornton Hall. Does that make a difference to you?"

He swept her into his arms and began kissing her, first gently and then more and more passionately. When they stopped for breath he said, "Does that answer your question?" He pulled her into a closer embrace as he whispered in her hair, "Ruby, my own precious Ruby." Then he pulled back for a moment and reached into his vest pocket. He pulled out a small leather pouch and in the palm of his hand lay a beautiful golden ring. It had a deep red ruby surrounded by a ring of diamonds. He placed it on her finger saying, "It was my mother's. My aunt found it in her trunk when I was in Ireland."

"It's beautiful, Peter, and fits my finger perfectly."

"Now I have one, perhaps temporary, condition. Caitlin is living with me right now and has nowhere else to go–" He gave her a questioning look, started to explain further but Ruby cut him off.

"— Of course I don't mind Caitlin living with us and she must stay as long as she likes. And I have always loved Linden Hall, for it is surrounded by those heavenly linden trees."

"We should plan to marry when they're in blossom,"

Peter said. "That will give me time to get the house prepared for you. There is still quite a lot to do."

"I don't mind renovations, Peter. But I have a condition, too."

"You have a condition for me?" he said, puzzled.

"I need you to understand that I love to bake. I learned as a child with my mother. Both my father and my Aunt Ada say that ladies don't bake. But I'm not quite a lady and I do. Will that embarrass you?"

"It won't embarrass me, not at all, Ruby. If you promise to be mine for all time, my lovely 'not quite a lady' wife can bake to her heart's content."

The End

A word about the author

Helena Korin

I was born in the magical city of Prague in the Czech Republic, once known as the Paris of central Europe. I love old architecture, opera, classical music and vintage clothing. Perhaps latent memories of my childhood are responsible. I have a degree in history and enjoy ferreting out obscure details of the lives of men and women who lived in centuries past. Writing about the Regency is my form of time-travel.

Contacts:
Friend me on Facebook
Follow me on twitter
Join me on Goodreads

Afterword

Thank you so much for reading my story, *Not Quite a Lady*. I had fun creating a heroine who loved to bake and wasn't a true aristocrat. In a book about the architecture of English country houses I found a reference to a dairy maid who married an English lord, in 1825. He was a friend of the Prince Regent. This sparked my imagination.

I'd love to keep in touch with you so please do me the honour of signing up for my occasional newsletter.

Helena

Newsletter